THE NEON YAK

ROBERT GARNHAM

THE NEON YAK

Liminal Ink from **Stoat Books**

First published in the UK in 2025

Stoat Books, Plymouth

Text © Robert Garnham

ISBN: 978-1-0683119-8-7

First Edition

The rights of Robert Garnham to be identified as the author
of this work has been asserted by Stoat Books.

1

1

Have you ever fallen asleep lulled by sirens on the distant motorway, or been mesmerised by electric flashes from late night trains? I remember how it used to be when I was a kid. The moment I closed my bedroom door, I felt as if I were in another world. We lived in the suburbs. The city was out there, the capital city with its skyscrapers and offices, and one night I was listening to the radio before going to bed, letting my thumb move the dial on my cheap battery-powered personal stereo and finding a station that was playing classical music, and listening to those strings and those woodwinds and the sawing rhythms and thinking just for a split second that the music was being played only for me. I thought that the orchestra had been sitting there waiting for me to tune in, because that's how magical the capital city could be. It knew everything. It was like God was supposed to be. The moment I closed my bedroom door, I felt its presence, and this would make me very nervous.

Through the distant crack of long wave, I'd hear electric storms out there on those hot humid nights. Each zap of lightning would interfere with the signal and crackle up the music. *There's a storm coming*, I'd whisper. And then I would look out of my bedroom window at those voluminous clouds lit up within by sheet lightning. My window faced east, right over the city. We lived on a hill just beyond the airport. If you go to the airport, you can see the hill in the distance, but you wouldn't necessarily know that people lived on top of it because it just looks like a wooded hill.

I remember those nights very vividly, even now. I remember one night I'd turned my lights off so that nobody could see my leaning on the windowsill. I could not *see* the capital city, but I could *sense* it, beyond our village suburb and down the hill and across the river and beyond the airport's runways. The other kids at school had been awful that day. Some of the boys in my class had got it into their heads that I wanted to be *posh*, and at playtime they had been chanting *posh boy, posh boy, posh boy*. This had made me embarrassed because for a start I didn't really want to be the centre of attention like that, and secondly, I wasn't posh, and I didn't want to be posh. We all lived on the same council estate. Why did they want to concoct a distance between us when we all lived at the same place? My fingertips sweated as I held on to the windowsill. I didn't know it at the time, but what came across as an aspiration to what they termed 'posh' was just the campiness of my mannerisms.

'Wow', I said, as the storm moved closer.

The lightning flashed, and it silhouetted the rows of identical houses that I could see from my window. I clung on to the windowsill as if I were on the bridge of a ship. I could see my reflection in the dark of the window, which I didn't like at all. I looked so average, and I looked so weedy. If I weren't so average and so weedy then I'd have a much, much, much more outgoing personality, and the stars would dance, and the universe would implode, and the end titles would roll, and the theme music would play. I plucked up the courage to look myself in the eye but at that exact moment another flash of lightning almost made me jump backwards from the windowsill, and it felt, yes, it really did feel as if the city were punishing me for wanting that moment of intimacy with myself.

'You're such a wimp, Danny Cooper'.

I'd said this to myself. It was a consolation because nobody ever called me *Danny*. Nobody called me *Dan*, either. I was Daniel then and I'm still Daniel now, because that extra syllable implies precision.

'Come on', I whispered, when there hadn't been any lightning for a while.

Perhaps the storm wasn't going to come this way. I'd not heard any thunder yet. It was probably just reserved for the

7

people in the city. I was wearing the headphones which were plugged into my little radio, headphones which had a kind of sponge padding, and the sponge padding would become damp the more I wore them on those hot nights. And the strings were sawing away, and the concert was building up to some kind of esoteric crescendo which meant nothing to me, and I plucked up the courage to try and look at myself.

'You're so silly, aren't you?', I whispered to my reflection. I could sense where my eyes were, but I didn't want to look right into them. 'Everything's so new. You're getting taller and thinner, and your internal organs are rearranging themselves and your nervous system is as finely tuned as it will ever be and yet you have no sense of time. You're only just starting to exist'.

Posh boy posh boy posh boy.

I looked down, and I tried to see if there were any movement in the back garden of the house next door. It all looked dark, but I'd know soon enough because the kid next door was a pyromaniac, and he used to go out when everyone else was asleep and set fire to things. You can't really sleep properly when you think that the house is going to catch fire. I couldn't see him tonight.

Was that another flash of lightning? Or had it come from the one the suburban trains?

'Do you still believe in monsters?', I asked.

The pyromaniac was a monster.

The moment I closed my bedroom door I imagined that the rest of the universe had ceased to exist. There were always strange noises which I couldn't rationalise. Blame the airport, blame the motorway, blame the reservoirs and the river, blame the city. Blame the forest.

'Blame anyone but yourself, Danny Cooper!'

Daniel Cooper.

And that's what I remember, just that strange few minutes standing there at the window, watching the excitement of someone else's storm.

This short novel is mostly true, and it takes place the same year that the shuttle exploded. It takes place the same year that there was an explosion at Chernobyl. It takes place in the summer between middle school and secondary school. It takes place at the exact time that I started to realise who I was. It all happened forty years ago, now. This is the story of how I came to be.

2

Sly wet leaves like a dead dog's tongue.

Nobody knew of my private place, deep in the woods through a thicket of rhododendrons verdant enough to form their own oxygenised clouds. I crouched under the tangled branches, stepped over the roots once I was inside the plant's pungent embrace, feeling nature ooze from the peaty, bouncy earth still wet from the rain three days before. At least it was cooler here. I was shielded from the summer sun and the blue sky, and the aircraft from Heathrow, surrounded by the shiny leaves of this suburban jungle. Just me, and the spiders. How cunning I was!

After a while I emerged into a clearing hidden from the world, enclosed by fleshy green vegetation, a bare plot where an oak had once stood. There was a patch of grass where I could sit for a while and read paperbacks which gave fictionalised accounts of prominent plane crashes. And it would be quiet here, except for the planes themselves, and the background rumble of traffic on the motorway, and the occasional police siren signalling someone else's emergency.

And I thought about myself.

I was a stranger to the usual pursuits, the wilful shouting, and the same old lusts of others in my year. I'd never wanted to fight with anybody, or scare anybody, or score a goal. I wanted only to leave the noise of home, and the shouting and the music and the sheer humanity of the 'estate' and find my own peace in libraries or parks or at my grandmother's house, or here in this rhododendron hideaway. Yet at the same time I was aware that the quiet was never truly absolute, because of the motorway hum and the noise within. I turned a page in my book, and I tried to concentrate on every word.

This place never did me any good, though I'd been coming for the last few weeks. I'd never been one for nature, finding it too dirty, too gruesome, too primal to contemplate, and would much rather have been indoors, and my allergies played up whenever I was outside in the summer, but I was able to put up with all of this because of the peacefulness. And afterwards I knew I would regret finding this peace, because next door would be playing their music and the kids would be shouting in the street and it really didn't seem fair because I'd been so content, but for now, here I was, and all I had to think about was myself. And oh look, there's a red admiral butterfly. And oh look, there's a Boeing 747.

I often dream even now of secret paths, and of my intent being discovered even when I've done nothing wrong. At the time this helped make my solitude even more enthralling, more so than that which motivated my classmates, such as money, and sport, and fashion, and making out with girls. But I would dream of these quiet days, and I would take my hay fever medication, and I would slip out unannounced and this would make the whole thing feel like a transgression as if I were stealing the silence which was owed to people much more worthy than me.

It felt like I had stayed in my private place for hours, but my mind was apt to spiral out into nothingness. Easily distracted, I looked at the contrast between my bare legs and the green grass, concentrated on an ant crawling over my knee, listening to the sparrows in the overhanging trees, and because all of this took energy, I started to feel time elongate. Then a sensation of guilt kicked in. I shouldn't have been there. What if something happened? What if my parents worried that I had been in an accident? Didn't the world already think that I was strange? I wouldn't want to draw attention to myself by being any more different. Didn't I think that I was already peculiar?

A heavy sensation in the pit of my stomach came abruptly from nowhere. I would have to go home, literally face the music, to the gangs of name-calling kids and the pyromaniac next door. I would have to put down the book and crawl back through the rhododendrons and find the path through the woods and go home to the 'estate'. And I would have to return to being the version of myself that I presented to the world. There was no escape. I could only ever be who I only ever was.

3

the humdrum. the same old. [SEP]the logic.

Daniel Cooper, this is your history.

[SEP]the suburbs with all their suburban psyche ever so frightening never struck by lightning hardly ever fighting conservatory-clung backyard train line whistle-whip suburban suburban nothing. [SEP]the trains. [SEP]the quiet streets with their brown brick identical departmental uniformity. the planes.[SEP]

Daniel Cooper, this is your history.

[SEP]the A30. [SEP]the M25 with its orbital four-lane crawler-lane corridor lights strung round at night in their sodium glare like a string of pearls around London's chubby neck. [SEP]Junction 13, Staines.

Daniel Cooper, this is your history.

[SEP]the people in my class. [SEP]Paul. [SEP]Kevin. [SEP]Malcolm with the runny nose. [SEP]Other Paul. Mark. we had all grown up together.

Helen. [SEP]Natasha. all the girls.

the village green. [SEP]

Daniel Cooper, this is your history.

London. that it should be just out of reach. [SEP]out of reach of quivering fingers outstretched, never touching. [SEP]the airport with its terminals and taxiways and tower blocks and takeaways and taxi ranks and terrorists. [SEP]the planes with their jet range long haul and their sharp fins like shark fins negotiating Hounslow hangars like the opening scene in Jaws.

Daniel Cooper, this is your history.

[SEP] the ethos. [SEP] the memories. telling the same old story with its half-lies and masked lives, it's allegations and feigned surprise, hints and suppositions and nice tries, concealments and disagreements, corruptions of the honest in all its truth-stealing layer-peeling, nerve-breaking heart-rending action-defending comedy-depending occasionally-resplendent ancestor-descendent shelf-replenishment life of mine in which absolutely nothing happened.

Daniel Cooper, this is your history.

4

My bedroom was at the rear of the house looking out over everyone's back gardens. It was a ramshackle assortment of sheds and yards and washing lines and television aerials. It looked east, so that the sun would come up and fill the room with sunshine very early in the morning in the summer. It also faced London, so that you could see a permanent layer of brown, yellow pollution hanging in the air.

The 'estate' had been built next to a village called Englemede. But London's suburbs had reached out and grabbed Englemede and now there wasn't a gap between Englemede and the rest of London. Once it had been a separate entity, and I could see older buildings from my bedroom window that, many years before, had probably just been on the edge of a field with nothing but farmland and common land and forest beyond. Now they were sitting on the edge of the 'estate', where all the roads were named after the trees that had been hacked down to accommodate it.

My desk was next to the window, so I could look out and see what was going on as I tried to write, because I wanted to be a writer, and I could see the aircraft rising up above the council houses because the end of Heathrow's runways was not too far away. Some of the aircraft were very noisy back then, particularly the ones heading to Australia or the Far East, and they'd perform a tight turn right above our house, their wings dipped, the sun glinting from their metal fuselage.

The couple next door was having an argument. My bedroom shared a wall with their house, with what was obviously the smaller kids' bedroom, judging by the noise every night. The couple next door always sounded like they were having an argument because even when they spoke normally, they tended to shout. The man had a deep booming voice which had a hard edge to it, a typical East Ender with all those vowels which sounded like a cat in pain, and sometimes I would try to imitate the way that he spoke. I wondered if the smoke from their son's pyromaniac had done something to his vocal cords, or perhaps he was also a pyromaniac when he was a kid. They were shouting to each other now, though I couldn't hear the exact words. I was trying to write. It was hard to work out if it was an argument or not; it had the music of an argument, but it didn't seem to be building up to anything. They were just griping at one another. And I would wonder if they were just doing it because they knew that I was trying to write and that it was being conducted spitefully, as was the yelling and crashing from their kids who, ignoring the muffled argument of their parents, were running around and jumping and screaming, and all of this was going on and I had the pen poised above the paper but no words were coming, I couldn't hardly think, no words were coming at all, and it was all so easy and probably proper to blame the row coming from the house next door on my lack of progress.

Didn't they understand that I was trying to create a whole new world from nowhere, and that doing so was a form of mental gymnastics, didn't they realise that if they could only be quiet for a while, and stop threatening to burn down the house, then I might enrich the world with my imagination, and that the words would dance just for me?

I popped in some earplugs that I'd bought from the chemist. They managed to block the distinct words but did little to mask the intent, the emotion, and the crashing and banging from their kids. I could still hear the noise even through the foam earplugs, and it would add to the sound of the beating of my own heart, and I wondered if it would ever be truly possible to escape from noise even when my own heartbeat was adding to the cacophony. How could I ever write under these conditions? The words came out distorted, like the classical music concerts on the radio crackled by static from unsolicited storms. It was all so deeply unfair. The words just came out meaningless, and it was because of the noise. And then when the argument finally stopped and I couldn't hear the kids crashing around their bedroom, I would start to worry that their teenage son had set fire to the house.

I thought of my late grandfather. He had extra sensitive hearing and could hear things happening miles away. What would he have made of all this? I looked down at the page and the words I'd written, but none of them seemed to make any sense. I was trying to conjure a whole new world, but nothing had come. And all the time the traffic on the motorway had been rumbling, droning, sighing away, and the aircraft were flying overhead.

5

One day I levitated. And I swear that this is true.

It was a hot night, though weren't they all hot nights? There wasn't even the slightest of breezes to lift the net curtains away from the open window, through which I could hear distant music and the incessant motorway. So sticky, so humid, the night itself a fist curled ready to punch into midnight and the small hours. I could not sleep. I was lying on top of the sheets, wearing only my shorts but even so, a pool of moisture had gathered on my chest. My hair at the time with had a centre-parting so that fronds of it fell into my eyes, and when I pushed them back, I could feel that my hair was damp as it trailed through my fingers. I felt a bead of sweat roll down my face. I closed my eyes and put my hands to my side, and I wished that I were somewhere else.

And I swear.

I swear I lifted off from the bed, ever so gently as if scooped up in someone's arms. I lifted off from the bed and felt the damp sheets fall away. I felt nothing underneath me, and when I opened my eyes I saw the ceiling getting closer, the white stippled ceiling with its cracks like a road network leading towards the capital city of the electric light fitting, the stippled valleys lit by the sodium glow from outside getting closer and closer, and my arms were at my side and I felt like my nose at any moment would hit the ceiling, be pressed against it, that I would be squashed because gravity had suddenly forgotten how to behave, and the night was so hot and I was sticky and yet I was rested on air and I swear that this is true, I swear right now that this is true, but even I don't believe it.

And then the ceiling receded. The bed received me, damp and cool. The night sky was brown with pollution and the glow from all the streetlights of the motorways and the suburbs, and I thought, *in all of London, in all of that mega-big city, I bet nothing like this has happened to anyone else tonight,* which was an oddly comforting thought.

6

It is odd to look back on this in its full historical context. Society was not conditioned then for anyone who didn't fit in with the perceived moral majority. I had been told from an early age by family members, friends, schoolmates, visiting school assembly vicars, sweaty comedians, the newspapers, and the government, that it was not the proper thing to have feelings for anyone other than the opposite gender. In the name of comedy, such people were to be ridiculed, and this was the only right thing to do. It was the moral thing to do. Backs against the walls, lads! That was the usual playground taunt, and I laughed along, usually relieved if this taunt was not aimed at me. After all, I'd come from a long line of straight men. It was in the family.

The excitement I found in regarding the male form, therefore, I assumed was universal among all of my peers. I could see no harm in admiring the physicality of the shirtless, toned, well-constructed gentleman, and, by extension, wanting to spend the rest of my life with one such fine example, and love them, and be loved by them. It was the sort of thing you might do if you were also a man and a woman. The realisation that this sort of behaviour was very much frowned on caused me perhaps to overcompensate. Any moment now, I believed, heterosexuality would kick in and I'd find the woman of my dreams. Any day, now. Any moment. And I would tell the lads at school all about the girl that I'd spend eternity with and how I hoped she'd have nice legs, short hair, a flat, powerful chest, a boyish grin, beautiful eyes, no make-up, a winning smile, muscles, and a preference for men's clothing, because that's what I liked, that's the sort of girl I liked.

It was 1986.

I liked anything funny. But *I* didn't want to be the punchline.

I could feel that a change was coming. And any moment now, it would all kick in.

7

'If you close your eyes and imagine hard enough then you might see God.'

Sitting in assembly on a wooden gym bench next to the hatch where they served lunch. The Head Mistress implored us to visualise the unattainable, let us pray, man is made in His image, she said. But my God was a drag queen.

I would half-open my eyes. Rows of school kids pretending to be pious. The lower years had to sit on the cold floor.

God will speak to you when the time is right, the Head Mistress said. And you must accept Him into your heart.

'The vicar looks like he's asleep, doesn't he?', Tina said.

Who is Tina? Tina is someone I invented. I kind of like Tina, but then I would do, because she is a part of me. I invented Tina because I wanted to see what it was like to invent a character who I might write about, but no matter what I do, Tina just won't go on to the page and insists on living somewhere at the back of my mind. That's the only way that I could describe Tina's existence.

Tina wore a big bouffant black wig, a sparkly red sequin dress. She had a vodka martini in her hand. Her heavy-lidded eyes had long fake lashes. Dangling earrings, lots of make-up, an American accent. She was sitting on a chair at the side of the hall.

'Go away. I'm meant to be praying'.

'Honey, it's all nonsense'.

'But the Head Mistress might tell me off!'

'She doesn't know, babes. Even the vicar isn't listening to a word she's been saying'.

The vicar really did look like he'd fallen asleep.

'Don't call me *babes*. I'm a fella'.

'What should I call you?'

'Daniel Cooper'.

'What about *Danny*?'

There was another Daniel in my class. Everyone called him *Danny*. Nobody ever called me *Danny*. I felt like a Danny, but nobody ever called me *Danny*.

'Where did you come from, anyway?'

'Honey, you've got to worship someone, it might as well be me'.

'Isn't this somewhat sacrilegious?'

'Such a big word, my dear. And you're still in middle school. Now, pay attention. She's off again'.

Let us pray, the Head Mistress said. Dear Lord, blah blah blah.

'How do you wear those heels?'

'Years of practice and a childhood spent in my mother's shoes'.

'That's disgusting'.

'Is it, my dear?'

'Men shouldn't want to be women. That's wrong'.

'Oh, I don't want to be a woman, sweetheart. I know exactly who I am. It's true that some men do, and you must respect that'.

'But it's disgusting'.

'Says who?'

'Well . . .'.

'Go on'.

'Everyone!'

Blah blah blah, went the Head Mistress.

'Look at yourself before criticising others', Tina said. 'Geez, I can see I've got my work cut out with you'.

'The world is just so simple. I don't know why people can't just stop all this nonsense and be with who they're supposed to be with.'

Blah blah blah. Blah blah blah. Aaaaaa-men.

(Amen).

'Honey. You'll understand soon enough'.

8

When it was hot in the summer you could smell the tarmac melting and the creosote that the council had put on all the wooden fences, which were a slat design in which each slat had a triangular top, like wooden stakes, in case there were an influx of vampires. The smell used to remind me of the forest, the woods, sap and vegetation, but then it would become overpowering like the woods were getting their revenge, and all these wooden slats were reminding us of what they had once been.

Our house, and all the neighbouring houses, were at a junction, where one road joined another, and for some reason the council had put a roundabout at this junction, and in the middle of the roundabout was a solitary lamp post. All the houses in our part of the road faced this lamp post, like it was some kind of very plain totem pole. Cars kept hitting the lamp post because nobody expected a roundabout to be there, let alone with a lamp post in the middle of it, and there would be a big CLANG and down would come the lamp post, it was a regular occurrence.

Creosote and hot tarmac.

A few years before my teacher had been a young man called Mr. Scott. Of course, I didn't know that he was a young man at the time, because everyone seems old when you're young yourself. It was scary when they told us that our new teacher would be a man. People in other classes would ask what it was like having a man as a teacher because all of the other teachers were women, and everyone assumed that he would be very strict because he was a male teacher, filled with anger and eager to exact this vengeance. He was, though, deeply religious, which would have mixed well with the other staff at the school, in particular the Head Mistress. He had a print of *Christ of Saint John of the Cross* by Salvador Dali pinned above the blackboard, which was always very scary to look at with its weird angle and shadows and the use of light, as if he were looking down on whatever Mr. Scott was writing on the blackboard.

My Dad used to say that Mr. Scott was very camp, but I didn't fully know what this meant yet, as I'd had no other male teacher to compare him with and I didn't know what a male teacher should act like. My Dad also used to say that Mr. Scott walked as if he had a roll of linoleum under his arm, in a way that the comedians on TV used to mimic whenever they were impersonating effeminate men. And then I started to understand what Dad meant when he said that Mr. Scott was camp.

When it got really hot in the summer, the tarmac on the roundabout would melt, and someone had scrawled in it MR SCOTT IS A TOSSER, and this stayed there for maybe ten years or more afterwards, so that every time I would walk or cycle past the roundabout, I'd think of Mr. Scott.

People tended to get incredibly irritable on the estate when the weather became hot, and I remember one night I was trying to write when I heard raised voices. My bedroom looked out the back, but I went to the front bedroom, and I saw Jason from around the corner facing Paul from two doors down facing each other in the glow from the lamppost on the roundabout, and they were obviously very angry with one another.

I didn't know what it was about, and I still don't know even now, because none of the adults afterwards seemed to want to talk about it, but at the time I assumed that the argument was about a girl, because that seemed the only logical explanation.

It was fascinating to watch. I raised the net curtain and looked out so that I could get a better view. It was like watching a documentary, though why someone would make a documentary about Jason and Paul is anyone's guess. Both were using lots of swear words, the sharp edges of which bounced back from the surrounding houses, rat a-tat tat, I had the window open just a crack to hear them better. Other people had come out of their houses for a better listen, but I wasn't brave enough to do that, and I heard our front door open as my dad went out to have a better look. Some of the neighbours had come out into the road and were leaning against the wooden slats of the fences, arms folded, watching intrigued as Jason and Paul continued their pre-fight tirades.

I understood that whatever was happening was probably stressful for both of them, whether Jason had slept with Paul's girlfriend, or Paul had slept with Jason's, or maybe they'd not even gotten as far as sleeping with one another's girlfriends and were just arguing about the possibility of it. The roundabout had become a sporting arena, sponsored by MR SCOTT IS A TOSSER, and there was this sense that something incredible was about to occur, because who wouldn't want to stand up for their girlfriend?

I could tell that they were arguing for their future, for a life together and the good times that would likely follow, because I knew from bitter experience how stressful it was waiting for the heterosexuality to kick in, and that both Jason and Paul had probably gone through the same process and been rewarded with the requisite straightness and now someone else wanted to take it away from him, but on the other hand, perhaps one of them had been wrongly accused. And I knew what that felt like, having been, once or twice, and only half in jest, mistaken to be homosexual.

When the fighting started, it was not as exciting as television had always promised. Jason and Paul tried to throw punches at one another but their opposite number kept ducking or stepping out of the way, and at one point they kind of grabbed each other's shoulders and grappled for a little bit as if it were now a wrestling match, and there was lots of screaming and shouting and I thought that perhaps the girl they were fighting over really wasn't worth all the bother, because they weren't putting everything into this fight.

27

It was at this moment that Mr. Jenkins from across the street stepped in, and then along came Barry from also across the street, obviously Barry had wanted to step in first but only did so when Mr. Jenkins did. And Jason and Paul were separated, and now there was lots of swearing and pointing and threats which felt empty, and I was watching this the whole time from the upstairs window thinking that perhaps the show was now over.

But this is when the scuffles started. Because the neighbours that had been watching from their gates didn't take too kindly to a certain group of young men who had appeared from elsewhere on the 'estate'. It looked to me that the street was a mass of bodies, what with Jason and Paul and Mr. Jenkins and Barry and the neighbours standing at their gates and fences and now this group of four or five young men. There was shouting, and the lads tried to advance on Mr. Jenkins who was holding Jason back, they were crowded around Mr. Jenkins, and now more neighbours stepped in to defend Mr. Jenkins, which only caused more shouting and swearing, and I recognised one of the young men who had just arrived as Luke, who was a couple of years older than me and tall and thin, and he was shouting at Jason. Barry was using his physicality to help Mr. Jenkins, and now someone was trying to stop him from doing so, and now it looked like everyone in the road was either fighting or trying to stop fights, and Luke had taken his shirt off, which was an added bonus, and the lamp post in the middle of the roundabout kind of looked down on this surprising melee, and I tried to chart the progress of the shirtless Luke but he was flailing his fists and moving in and out of the throng, I suppose he wanted as many people as possible to see his smooth, powerful chest, and why not. Paul was now free and he was being pursued by Barry, and the Pyromaniac from next door was kind of leaning against his Dad's car as if he was waiting for it to all calm down before he could set fire to something, and all I could see from my vantage point at the upstairs window were figures moving around in the sodium glow, in slow motion, as if they were swimming. I watched entranced, and I wondered why I didn't want to go and join in, and my Dad was out on the street yelling at people to just pack it in and behave like adults, but everyone was ignoring him, and I found it all deeply fascinating and then a new feeling took over, that whatever happens in life, I have no control over anything.

When the solitary police car arrived with its flashing blue light, everyone seemed to scatter apart from the neighbours who were still leaning on their fences or standing in their doorways. Luke, I noticed, had the good sense to find his t-shirt and scoop it up before he went scampering off. An aircraft was flying overhead. What must its passengers have thought of this?

'Show's over', Tina said. 'My oh my! All that testosterone. . '.

'He was standing up for his girlfriend'.

'Honey, they were just getting things out of their system'.

I let the net curtain fall back, and I watched through it, as the policeman chatted to people who were still gathered.

'Getting what out of their system?'

For once, Tina did not have an immediate response. She thought about the question for a couple of seconds.

'Just . . . Everything', she sighed.

9

For years, carved in hot melted tarmac

In the suburban commuter town where I grew up, the words

Mister Scott is a Tosser

A permanent memorial to a teacher

Long since, having passed through, forgotten by most,

Gone.

His name a mystery to succeeding generations.

He lived in a flat tacked to the side

Of the church hall. I suppose it came with his job

In our C of E middle school.

The place might even have seemed exotic, bohemian

Divorced from the humdrum of growing up,

Though, a deeply religious young man,

Probably he disapproved of anything remotely bohemian.

A bachelor.

My dad said he walked as if he had

A roll of lino under his arm.

Jutting chin, and the Alex Hurricane Higgins hairstyle

Of the early 1980s.

Was Mister Scott a tosser? No, he was reasonable.

He encouraged me to write, and for that,

I shall never inquire as to what he got up to

In his church hall bachelor pad,

Scene of nativity plays and jumble sales,

Whether tossing or not.

10

A weak sun forced itself through the early morning mist and burned off the malaise. The air was suffused with the smell of aviation fuel. The common land, of gorse bush and heather with patches of grass, fern, clumps of trees, swamps, and ponds, stretched away and revealed itself as the mist lifted. The motorway was close, hiding in its culvert and growling with its mysterious anger. The bigger lorries sigh, they don't want to do whatever is being asked of them, but they do it anyway. I'd chained my bicycle to a notice a couple of miles back which said, *No Campfires*. Aircraft passed overhead unseen in the fog.

There were paths marked out across the common land, and others which only existed because people had wandered. The paths were slow going because they were made just of sand, and the sand got into my sneakers and made walking uncomfortable. Wet bushes brushed against my bare legs, and the mist made me feel muggy and awkward. I didn't know why I had gone there because I was not enjoying any of it. As I walked along the landscape disappeared behind me as the fog folded in, like the sun had been defeated in trying to burn it off and it was now coming back, the fog was returning. It felt like I was walking in a mysterious void, though the common was just a gap between towns, between suburbs, and designated as a site of special scientific and environmental interest because those stunted gorse bushes were home to some rare butterflies or frogs or species of lizard.

The main thing for me was that it was quiet there. How was I ever going to be a writer if I was surrounded by so much noise? Beautiful words, sentences sublime and the eternal dance of literature cannot be conjured from the ether in the back bedroom of a cacophonous council house. My world was a noisy place, and writers are a rare species, just like those rare butterflies on the common, and they exist only in quiet places. They exist in pockets of solitude and contemplation where they can coax narratives and storylines out into the open and then on to the page. It couldn't possibly happen in my bedroom, not in that house, not surrounded by all that shouting. I shouldn't have picked up a pen in the first place. I shouldn't even have bothered. I was surrounded by too much noise.

I bent down and I took my sneakers off. Granules of sand were irritating my feet as I walked. I took my socks off, too, and walked along in the cool sand unencumbered. It felt like I was now connected to the planet in a tactile kind of way, the sandy path soft and cushioning every step. It felt like I was at the seaside. And now the fog was closing in again. It was like I finally had a quiet room of my own that followed me around as I walked, and the walls were made of fog.

In the days following the argument in the street I'd started to feel very wary about things. It was weird because I'd felt fine while watching the altercation, but the effects it had, had started to come afterwards. Small things had started to perturb me, and whenever I heard a loud noise, I thought that it was all starting up again. Sudden movements, or car doors opening or closing, both had me rushing to the window and peering out, half-hidden on the other side of the net curtain. The screaming of the kids next door matched another kind of screaming. An internal screaming, perhaps. But then I would tell myself that I was getting too wrapped up in my own existence and that other people had it much worse than me.

So, I was barefoot on the common. I had no idea how far I was from the main road or from my bicycle, now. A smaller path went off at a tangent to the side, and I took it, wondering if this led to the pond. My idea was to go there and read for a while and then take out my notebook and my pen and try to do some writing. It would be quiet at the pond, apart from the occasional walker and the aircraft flying overhead and the sound from the motorway, but it was a Monday morning with no school because of a teacher's training day, and most people would be at work. Nobody would be stupid enough to come out here on the common in this increasingly thick fog with the sun now barely able to make its way through.

Strange shapes swirled all around me. I stopped for a while, and the ground started to feel very cold as I sank down a little bit into the sand. The gorse bushes had little spikes on them. In the summer, the broom bushes had seeds on them which would pop open when the sun was out, you could hear them popping away if you were sitting near to them. The way that the fog now curled around was creepy. The shapes that I could see were just the gorse bushes and the heather, they were barely visible. I could still taste the pollution.

My Dad would tell me about the pea-souper fogs that they had when he was a kid growing up in London. This felt more like a chicken-souper. It was kind of yellow.

I'd brought some books to read, and I would sort out which one to read once I got to the pond. I was starting to become jealous of all the characters in the fiction books that I was reading, because they were all insistent in droning on about their lives but none of them mentioned being affected by noise. Heathcliffe was pining for his Cathy, but it was probably nice and peaceful up there on the Yorkshire Moor. Hemingway's Old Man was busy fighting his big fish in the middle of the sea, but you could bet that nobody was playing a deep-base party music album nearby. Didn't any of these writers understand what real people had to go through in their lives? At least I had my book of fictionalised accounts of famous plane crashes to fall back on.

I must have been getting close to the pond. I never knew the name of the pond, and not many people knew that it was there. An elderly neighbour, who's dead now, once walked his dog near the pond and it was bitten on the nose by an adder. The adder curled around the dog's nose and bit it. The dog had to go to the vets, and it was fine after a while. That's about the only thing the pond represented for me at that time. I thought that perhaps when I got there, I'd wade into the pond itself at the shallowest part and feel the cold water and let it take all of the sand granules away from the soles of my feet, and nobody would be able to see me because of the fog.

'Honey, you just gotta do what feels good'.

Tina had been behind me the whole time, walking awkwardly in her high heels which sank down into the sand. There was an expression on her face of deep discomfort. It wasn't her thing at all, to be outside and to be surrounded by nature. She almost spilled her vodka martini.

'I always do'.

'You're just saying that, dear, because it sounds good in the saying'.

'OK, sometimes I don't . .'.

Because I had to admit that it all felt good, now. Walking here, on the common, in the fog, feeling the sand between my toes, it all felt good. It didn't feel good when I started because it didn't seem like the sort of thing I normally did, but now it felt good. Because I was away from the house and the noise and the potential violence and perhaps once I got to the pond I'd take out my notebook and my pen and I'd let the words come calling and I'd write something truly magnificent. And I'd be able to concentrate, for once. Nothing would be disjointed or distracting. And the fog, that thick muffling fog, made everyone's comprehension of the world just that little bit more complicated, which suited me just fine. It made the world a little more equal.

I must have been near the pond, now. I could see the trees which surrounded it, or at least, I could make out their shape in the gloom. But what was this? A lone blue light in the distance, flashing. Flash, flash, flash. A sprite, perhaps, or a willo' the wisp? Flash, flash, flash. Instinctively, I put my sneakers back on, just in case I had to run.

There were more shapes ahead, but these weren't gorse bushes or heather, and they weren't trees or saplings, or anything else. They were moving. They were humanoid. People! There were three of them, right on the edge of where the pond should be. One of them was standing with his hands on his hips. The other two were bent over, looking at a shape on the ground. Another shape, a silhouette puppet, lying in the gloom. Perhaps they were telling it to wake up. Was it a homeless person, or a drunk? The two shapes to the left picked this shape up at either end. A stretcher, with a body lying on it. That's what it looked like. That's definitely what it looked like. I could just make out their uniforms, for they were policemen and ambulance drivers. The figure with his hands on his hips looked up.

'Hey kid', he said. 'You'd better not come any closer. Turn around and go back'.

I didn't say a word. I just did exactly as he had said.

11

I didn't want to tell anybody what I had seen. For a start, I was worried what my family would have said if I'd told them that I'd been going to the common. People in the suburbs aren't very adventurous and if I'd have said, 'I'm going to the common to read a book and do some writing', then instead of saying, 'Oh, how wonderful, you can read in silence and write all you like out in a place like that, and let your imagination drift', instead of saying all that, they'd probably just say, 'What on earth for?'

It was almost time to break up at school and then it would be the summer holiday, and then I would be going to secondary school. Middle school was an eight-classroom cluster of low-level buildings in Englemede, but the secondary school was huge, and it was nearer to the airport, and it had several different buildings and about two hundred classrooms and a big tower block which was also full of classrooms and science labs and a gym, and each of the years had about ten tutor groups, and there were four years at the school. I was not looking forward to it.

During that last week at middle school, we had an assembly. 'You may have noticed', the Head Mistress said, 'That Charlotte has not been at school this week'. Charlotte was in a class two years below my year. 'Unfortunately, her mother has passed away. I have been given permission by her family to tell you this. And I want us all to pray for her family, and for Charlotte, and for her older brother, Luke, who is currently at the secondary school. We must all pray for these poor people in their time of loss. Because it is all a part of God's master plan'.

Naturally, I wondered if this Luke was the same Luke that I knew from the 'estate', the one who had taken off his shirt during the fight.

At break time the talk was all about the girl whose mother had died, and there were rumours that she had drowned herself in the pond on the common, and that she had done it on purpose, and I thought, how weird, because I was only there the other day, and someone had also drowned, and that it must be the latest thing to go to the pond on the common and drown yourself. Of course, it didn't cross my mind that they might have been the same person.

12

The world was a confusing place back then, so much so that I really didn't know when to apply any sort of sensitivity. Empathy was not one of my strongest traits. The universe moved in a certain way, and I believe it did so with a purpose, as if people's actions and the consequences of those actions were always worked out by them in advance and therefore came as no surprise to them. Charlotte, the girl whose mother had drowned herself in the pond, registered to me just as a fact, and I didn't once think why or ponder how sad it must have been for her, for this to have happened to her mother. It was an event which had occurred. Yet at the same time, I excused for myself this sense of purpose that I saw in other people. If I did something and it went wrong, like propping my bike against the wall outside a shop and the bike falling over or dropping a book that I was reading, then this happened entirely because I didn't have this sense of purpose. And I was excused this because I was me, and nobody else was.

One of my favourite places to go was the library in the next town. It was quieter there, and warm, and it had large modern windows which let the light flood in, and it had comfortable chairs between the rows of shelves, and study tables scrawled with graffiti from the students at the sixth form next door.

I would go there whenever I could and I would try to write, and I'd concentrate on what I was writing, and I'd feel this trance-like state in which the world around me would disappear, and I'd find myself living in the story that I was working on.

How ethereal were these afternoons! As my pen glided across the narrow-ruled lines of the file paper, I'd feel another part of my brain drift off into a mesmerising state in which time itself seemed not to exist. It was a sensation which felt so very pleasant that I wondered if this is what it felt like to take drugs or become high or to get drunk. The world had these sudden fuzzy corners, and I could feel my soul skipping along ever so slightly above reality, the same way that the words on the page skipped ever so slightly above the lines of the file paper. It was a feeling I didn't ever want to stop. As the afternoon wore on to the sounds of the librarians using their date stamps, or the whirr of the photocopier, I'd write until I had an abrupt sense of dread that I'd have to go back home soon.

Despite this, in actual terms, I was so remarkably insensitive.

I cared about my own senses. But not those of the people around me. I hope that I am different now.

One day that summer, as I was writing in the library, I half-acknowledged that one of the librarians was in the next aisle. She was an elderly lady with one shoe that was built up with a big block, that she always walked with a limp. She must have had some kind of medical episode while I was writing, because she leaned against the wall and slowly slid down it until she was sitting on the floor with her legs in front of her. And all I could think was, *oh, she's having a little sit down*, and I carried on with my writing.

It didn't cross my mind, and I'm glad, because if it had, I'd have been angry with her for interrupting my concentration. It didn't even register that she might have been taken ill. I just thought that she was having a little sit down. After a while she was discovered by one of her colleagues and she was helped to her feet, but I really wasn't taking much notice. I was too busy writing.

I didn't understand the way that the world worked. Which isn't a good thing when you want to be a writer.

13

I wanted to create for myself a delicate existence. I liked to skim across the surface of life. I drew back the curtains of my window and watched another Boeing take to the sky, rising from behind the older houses at the end of the street. These houses were built before the airport was even there. They had red tile roofs and chimney pots, and sash windows, and they looked tired and droopy, and their television aerials all faced the same way as metal birds all watching the same event. They used to be right on the edges of the fields, these old houses, but now they looked out at the 'estate'. Soon the Concorde would take off and then it would crack the afternoon wide open with its afterburner glow and it would see the curvature of the earth. And I'd still be sitting in the same place.

The pyromaniac was in his back garden. He had what looked like a strip of rags, the sort that his father has been using when he was working on his car out in the street round the front. The strip of rag was coated in oil from the car's engine. The pyromaniac flicked a lighter, flick, flick, flick, and set fire to the bottom of the piece of rag, which he then held from the top with a pinched finger and thumb. He watched as if mesmerised as the flames worked their way up the piece of rag almost to his fingers. At last, he dropped it on the ground when the heat became too much and he stamped out the flames, then looked down at it, then looked up at me in my window. He gave me the finger, then ambled off.

I feel so thin. I feel so insubstantial. All the proper men are much bigger than me.

Another aircraft took off. Where was the Concorde? When it comes it will split the afternoon sounding like a sore throat, scratchy and roaring. Dream visions of aerial joy. This next plane was another boring Boeing, heading west Atlantic-bound, some Pan Am grey for the psyche. How quickly did they fly from the throb of next door's music?

I'd taken to wearing earplugs to drown out their music. It would have made them so mad if they knew that their music didn't have any effect on me! But it did, because the base beat infiltrated the foam of my earplugs, like a heartbeat, as if I were in the belly of a whale. So then I took to grinding my teeth in order to fill my head with my own noise, my own base beat, which I did irrespective of their playing music or not, because it masked whatever the truth may have been. Grinding my teeth was wearing my canines down into sharp points, like I'd become a vampire.

If Tina were there in the room with me, she'd have been sitting on the edge of my bed, her fishnet-clad legs folded awkwardly in front of her, the smell of her perfume wafting, wafting.

Here it comes!

You hear Concorde before you see it. You sense it. A roar on the runway like a lion, an earthquake for the soul, and finally it becomes visible as a swooping shrouded cobra slithering the smog, a small metal dart ahead of its own sound with a barrage that pulverises the moment, judders the windowpane, the floorboards, masks unsolicited music, causes pedestrians to pause mid-stride, conversations to stop mid-sentence, for they cannot compete, it lifts higher and cracks open the day's pollution, rockets skywards does this monster with unusual haste, and then, oh then, it has gone.

Everything else was normal after the Concorde had gone.

14

'I'm just a poor girl from the wrong side of the tracks', I imagine Tina saying to me.

'I'd better stay away from you, then'.

We were walking through the 'estate' to the local shop. To buy milk.

'Honey, what side of the tracks were you born?'

'Nowhere near the railway lines. Watch out for that dog shit'.

The sound of Tina's heels echoed back from the surrounding houses.

'The sky lights up at night, though, doesn't it? When the trains get to the points further down the line. The sky flashes, doesn't it? Electricity, like the flashbulbs of all those cameras that used to wait for me outside nightclubs and fashion events. I'm used to it, though. Someone's society wedding? Hey, let's invite Tina, she'll get the party going. Darlings, I say to the cameramen, the paparazzi, make sure to catch my best side'.

'I thought you were a poor girl . . '.

'Babes, I was. But I raised myself up, didn't I? Through hard work, you know what I mean, wink-wink'.

'What kind of hard work?'

'Slow down, dear. I'll spill my martini'.

'Some people are just lucky'.

'It could happen to anyone. But a lot of the time, you've got to make your own luck. Look in the mirror and ask, *do you really want to go on like this?*'

'Like what?'

'Your mother was speaking to you this morning and you didn't hear a word that she said because of those damn earplugs'.

'I find them necessary'.

'And how are your teeth?'

'A little sharp'.

'Darling . . .'.

Tina had stopped. She had her left hand on her hip. Her right hand still held the martini glass. She gave me a withering glance and then took a sip.

'Darling, that behaviour ain't normal'.

'Well . . .'. I thought about my comeback for a couple of seconds. 'Well, you're not normal'.

I'd had enough of her. I turned around and started walking faster, knowing that she could not keep up in her heels. I could not understand why she was so interested in my life and felt it so important to point out certain faults when she was parading about in a ruby red sequin dress and a big black wig. Some people were weird. Let me get used to my own life, first, I felt like saying to her, before you pile in with your own suggestions. Do I not get a chance to grow familiar with myself?

2

15

Grandmother lived in the forest.

She lived in what had once been a two-up two-down Victorian brick cottage in the woods on a hill which was on such high ground that you could see it from Heathrow Airport. Englemede was also on a hill, but you couldn't see it from Heathrow Airport because of the houses and the smog, but Grandmother's house was five miles from Englemede. It was surrounded by trees. It always felt special.

Grandmother had difficulty walking then, so she only used the rooms downstairs. Even though it had been built as a two-up two-down cottage, over the years people had kept adding rooms onto the back of the ground floor. So it had slowly become a kind of disorganised maze of rooms one added on to the next. What had been the outside coal bunker was now inside because the rest of the house had engulfed it, and now the coal bunker had been painted pink, and it was the bathroom. Three flagstone steps led down from what had once been the back door to the kitchen. This led to the toilet, which had once been an outside toilet but now the ground floor had engulfed it too during the Victorian era and it was also inside. If you were in the front room and you needed to go to the toilet, then you had to pass through six rooms, and open and close six doors.

Nanna did not use the front room until after she had had her evening meal. She spent the early part of the day in what had once been the original kitchen, but it was now another kind of sitting room. It was unheard of to go to the front room until after seven o' clock.

My parents decided that once school had broken up, I should go and spend a few days with my grandmother. I acted nonchalant about the idea but inwardly I was pleased because I knew that it would be quiet there, because grandmother's house was in the woods and the only sound would be the birds, if you ignored the constant rumble of traffic on the motorways and the noise of aircraft taking off. I left with a backpack stuffed full of clothing and a couple of books to read and all my writing things and I thought that it might be quite relaxing to be surrounded by silence for once.

Grandad had died a couple of years before. Grandad was a gentle and quiet man, who always wore a tie and thick black glasses so that he reminded me of a television comedian. He had a workshop at the bottom of the garden. It was a corrugated iron shack about the size of a small house, or so it seemed to me when I was a kid. It seemed enormous, and it seemed like another world. And in this workshop, he would invent tools to do the sorts of jobs that no-one ever thought about until they needed to do those jobs and needed a tool to do it. Like killing slugs or attaching washing lines to the walls of a house without a ladder. And in his workshop were a lathe and a drill and lots of little drawers filled with screws and bolts, and a workbench, and a little window, and it was surrounded by trees, and grandad would always make me stand at a safe distance as he was operating his machinery because of all the rubber belts and drills and cogs but he would let me watch him create substance just from ideas that were in his head, and now I suppose I was doing the same but with words.

But grandad was gone, now. And grandmother was on her own, and this is another one of the reasons why my parents thought that it might be a good idea for me to go and stay with her. They felt guilty that she was on her own. They thought I might give her some company for a while. It would be good for the both of us.

16

I told them I felt

happy there.

Mother replied,

That's the spirit

of your great grandmother.

She made everyone

feel welcome.

Always a smile on her face,

a loving word,

the sheer joy of life

in a sunbeam

yellow gold.

It felt

and smelled

like a church.

Mould spores,

my dad pointed out,

rising damp,

subsidence.

17

The weather changed to torrential rain. No more the sunshine of the weeks leading up to the school holiday. It clattered in a relentless deluge on the roof of the back porch, where Grandmother grew cuttings and kept her rarer plants. It pelted the foliage of the surrounding woods and dripped constantly from the holes in the old iron guttering next to my bedroom window. Grandmother lit the ancient gas fire in the middle room. It had been installed where the old coal oven had once been, and as the gas flames popped and fizzed, and as Grandmother's hearing aid whined ever so softly. I sat back in Grandad's old easy chair as she told me of days gone by.

Grandmother reminded me of one of those old clockwork toys that didn't stop until it was completely run down, but you could sense when the energy was starting to go. In her slow, carefully enunciated voice, she would recall tales involving people I'd never met in places I'd never been. Her former neighbour, who'd worked as a glazier at the lunatic asylum, worked all day replacing the windows broken by those who were staying there and would think nothing of replacing the exact same window two, three, four times a day. The friend from her childhood who had bragged that she was going on holiday to a very posh cottage in Devon, only to arrive and discover that it was a converted pig pen.

She pronounced all her words carefully as if it were quite an effort to get them out into the open, and from the depths of her memory would come so many stories from years past. And as she told these stories, the gas fire popped, and rain pelted the back porch roof, and my mind would wander and I would think, *I'm sitting in the middle of a forest.*

'When I was a girl, my father – your great grandfather – became the manager of a hotel next to the railway station. So, we closed up this house and we moved there for a year as he managed the place, which he was only doing for as a favour for a friend. He was heavily involved with the church, your great-grandfather. He was in the choir. Every Sunday we would dress in our finest clothes, and we would go to the church, and my father would sing . . '.

I felt comfortable being there with my grandmother. As she spoke, I began to wonder what she thought of me, and whether she thought I were odd, or whether she felt a sense of sorrow that her daughter now lived on the 'estate' in the next village, and how good it was to have this fairytale tumbledown house in the woods whereas her daughter and her daughter's family lived in a wilderness of another kind entirely. Did she see me as a product of that wilderness?

'Your grandfather undertook a chauffeuring course in London. They showed him how to drive and how to treat their clients. They also learned about motor mechanics. That's why he was so very good at looking after motorcars. He was very mechanically minded, your grandfather. His father was a park ranger . .'.

I realised that I hadn't been listening to what Grandmother had been saying, that her words were just sounds that were washing over me like music because they were the only noise that I could hear rather than the usual noise I was used to, and that this was very sad because she was old, and she might never speak some of these words ever again.

She was now talking about a television personality who had recently been in a scandal which all the newspapers were talking about. She was saying that he had been one of her favourite television personalities, a light entertainer who made her laugh with his antics and his silliness, but now he was scandal-ridden and was on the front pages of all the newspapers because of something vile that he was supposed to have done. Everything was different, she said, because he had had to make a startling revelation about himself during this scandal, and I flinched because I knew what was coming and I knew that Grandmother would take ages to pronounce the word slowly, carefully, lingering over every syllable. The television personality is a *ho-mo-sex-u-al*. It took her several seconds to say the word, and I flinched, I flinched because I was used to living with a family and with friends who would now use that word as an excuse to spit their innermost bitterness, justify their hatred, and affirm their resolute opposition to such a thing. Yet instead, she merely said, in her slow and very careful voice, that she hoped he felt better now, and more at peace with himself that he no longer needed to hide away from the world.

Her attitude towards the television presenter shocked me. Everyone knew the story, and everyone needed to pile in, on the playground or around the dinner table with various uncles and explain in detail why this television presenter should be shunned, arrested, imprisoned, forgotten about. But Grandmother saw beyond this. And it shocked me. Before I knew what I was doing, I had to blurt out that it was all absolutely disgusting and that he should be ashamed of himself.

We all can't be the same, now, can we, was her response.

She said it so calmly. And then we just listened to the rain, for a while.

18

Neon Yak came shimmering through the saplings, electric flanks pulsing in the gathering dusk. A hoof pawed the ground sending up sparks which fizzled the undergrowth. His red eyes bore into the copse, gave shadows to the ferns, and these shadows swayed with the movement of his head. No lucky humans tonight will benefit from his presence, for he is unnoticed, unbothered, in the randomness of his manifestation. Just the hedgehogs and the deer, the bats, the trees. There are not enough Neon Yaks in the world, and their power is limited only to the one soul each day who must use their glimpse wisely and embrace whatever opportunity has been handed to them. The Neon Yak is conscious that people yearn for a sighting of him. He does not seek contact, though he doesn't go out of his way to avoid it. For such is all a question of luck, and there have been plenty of tales over the years of those whose fortunes have improved immeasurably after such a viewing. But they must, as a price, cede a part of themselves. Nobody ever comes away from a sighting as quite the same person. They all had to undergo this transformation.

19

Grandmother advised against going for a walk in the woods on account of the rain and said that I would catch a cold. She didn't understand that colds don't work that way. She also didn't understand that the rain would make such a walk more of an adventure, and how nice it would be to come back to the house afterwards to warm up, and get dry, and feel cosy. 'You know best', she said, 'I'll just sit here in the dry and I'll read my book.'

I imagined Tina would keep her company. Tina would sit in Grandad's old armchair, her long legs stretched out in front of the gas fire, her red sequin shoes reflecting the popping flames.

'Knock yourself out, kiddo', she would say, raising her martini glass.

Grandmother's house was on a hill, but not at the very top. The top of the hill was covered in woodland, and I knew that the first thing I would want to do was to walk to the very top of the hill. The second thing I wanted to do was to go and look for the Special Stone.

Both, of course, were dependent on whether or not I saw the Neon Yak.

I wasn't a superstitious person. But as I put on my plastic mac and walked out of Grandmother's front door, and walked across the road and into the woods, I could not stop thinking about the Neon Yak. It had been the talk of the playground for a couple of weeks after one of our year swore blind that he had seen the Neon Yak while out in the woods with his elder brother, and that nothing bad had happened, for the Neon Yak was a harbinger of change. Whoever happened to glance at its phosphorescent flanks as they sidled between the trees would find their lives to be altered in ways incomprehensible even to consider. Nobody wanted to see the Neon Yak unless they wanted their lives to change.

Yet the idea of its manifestation excited me. As far as I understood it, the world was an unchanging place and I would have to adapt to being a part of it, knowing that at any moment my heterosexuality would kick in and that I would live a happy and full life. Even so, the change I required to do this was too insurmountable just for one person to handle, so maybe a sighting of the Neon Yak would be beneficial. Stranger events had recently occurred to me. Hadn't I once levitated?

The rain was relentless. It clattered around me on the undergrowth, the bracken and the ferns and the brambles. Once into the woodland proper, though, the canopies of the trees above went some way to lessen the impact of the deluge to such an extent that I was able to remove my hood as I started to climb to the top of the hill, which helped if I was going to keep a lookout for the Neon Yak. The ground was a sponge-like mix of dead leaves and mulch, mud, moss and tree roots waiting to trip the inattentive. Rabbit holes. Gullies.

When I was younger my Grandad would take me for walks in the woods and we would listen out for the different birds, and I'd always drag a stick behind me, gathering leaves in my wake. He'd take me to the Special Stone, a large boulder surrounded by trees in the middle of the woods, which he'd lift me on to. Once I'd got to the top of the hill, I'd go looking for the Special Stone.

The going was steep. I tried to run up the hill, but it hurt the muscles in my legs to do so. This was the first time that I'd ever walked in the woods on my own, but it didn't feel like I was on my own because of the rain. At last, I reached the top of the hill, and only now did I give myself the pleasure of turning around to look at the view.

I could see the whole of London. Why hadn't I noticed this the other times I'd come? Why had nobody pointed this out to me? Because I'd not yet learned to see anything beyond the immediate. Perhaps Grandad hadn't been interested in pointing out the view of the city in which he'd learned to be a chauffeur. Or perhaps I'd just been too ignorant when he'd tried to show me. But there, through the trunks of the trees, I could see all the way across the city, from Heathrow to the Telecom Tower, and the NatWest Tower, the usual smog-filled air cleansed by the rain. And I stood there, and I gawped at this place in whose gravity I'd been orbiting since the day I was born, in whose suburbs my family had lived and loved and worked, in whose polluted air I'd dreamed so often of escape.

I did not see the Neon Yak. Seeing the capital made up for this. I never knew, I whispered to myself. *I never knew it was visible from Grandmother's house.* The house my mother grew up in. Why didn't anyone tell me? Why did nobody mention the magic? I looked down and I saw the slate tile roof of Grandmother's house and I wondered why nobody had ever given me this context before.

I walked down the hill in the direction that I remembered the Special Stone being. Yet the woods had become overtaken with thick brambles in the area where I knew the stone to be, and it would not be possible to thrash my way through. This was disappointing, and the rain started to become more insistent, so I had to put my hood up. The thorns and brambles had grown in the gap where an oak had obviously fallen in the last few years, which is why the rain was heavier here, because there was no canopy of leaves to protect me. I walked all the way around this clump of vegetation, stepping over brambles and creepers, and my behaviour must have looked very strange if anyone had been watching.

However, my efforts paid off, for I saw it a metre or so in from the edge of the undergrowth, half-covered by ferns and brambles and stinging nettles and soaked a dull grey by the rain. It was much smaller than I had remembered. The Special Stone, I thought, does not look quite so special anymore. Using my foot, I kicked the brambles away, made my way into the thick vegetation, and half-stood on the stone as if having just conquered an incredibly small mountain. And then I thought about my Grandad, and how much time had passed since we had been here together, and how I had grown taller and was no longer a little kid, and how I would very soon become a man and probably get married and have kids that he would never see, and it would all happen, irrespective of whether I saw the Neon Yak or not.

The ground was squelchy, and the undergrowth had made my trousers damp. The rain was pouring off my plastic mac. It was time to go back, now. Grandmother and Tina would both be waiting for me.

20

Grandmother went to bed early. Her bed was now in the corner of the front room because she could no longer climb up the stairs. She said that I could use the back bedroom, but I had to make the bed myself. It was weird being in a bedroom that was somewhere else because I still expected the noise, the music, the sound of screaming kids through the wall, but there was nothing because Grandmother lived in the woods. I still wore my earplugs, just in case.

It had finally stopped raining earlier in the evening, and the sky cleared, and once it got dark, the stars came out. I didn't care about the stars, because I could see the whole of London from the window. The capital just sat there, and as it became dark, all of its lights came on, and its neon, and I could even see the blue of the motorway signs lit up, and the yellow of the streetlights, and Heathrow's runway lights, and the tower blocks and the office buildings all lit up, and advertising hoardings, and the logos and it all just sat there shimmering through a heat haze, formless and just ever so slightly out of reach.

I had my small portable radio and foam over-ear headphones and as I looked at the city, I moved the dial over the radio stations on FM and I listened to snippets from each, as if I were trying to listen to the city itself. Pop songs and late-night jazz, political discussions, an opera, a concerto, and I wished that I had a telescope so that I could look down from my vantage point on a hill surrounded by trees and watch what was going on. It was all so very exciting, listening in on the very same city that I was looking at.

And all those lives sat there before me. A scratch of static and I heard violins. Crawl the dial across the ether, the violins disappear into a fuzz, and now someone's crooning, and somewhere out there in that mass of lights, other people were listening, too. What were all those people doing in their flats and their suburban houses and their shops and their cars, what were they thinking right at that moment? Of love, and money, or sleep, or politics, or books. How many people were sleeping right now? Were they looking at these dark wooded hills at this moment and thinking the same?

I started to feel hot. The world had warmed up since the rain stopped and now it was a muggy and uncomfortable nuisance. The trees held moisture in the air and soaked the night with a sweat like sap. I leaned my arms on the windowsill, leaned my forehead against the cool glass, and thought of my mother in this very same room growing up as a kid, when the city was much smaller and the lights not quite so bright. And then I thought of the blitz, the very same glass of this window a witness to bombs and fires and the searchlights and a demonstration of humanity's inhumanity. And now here was I, so incredibly insignificant in the greater scheme, elevated just for this moment as a city's witness.

I would never be able to engage fully with metropolitan life, so long as the developments my own psyche craved refused to occur. I strained my eyes to glimpse amid electric logos and advertisement billboards, the glowing form of the Neon Yak. But the Neon Yak is a creature of the woods, a local entity who haunts the hills and the trees, and cities are ever-changing, and urban souls have no need of such mythologies, for their world is built on artifice and fluctuation. My own life had been spent in the suburbs, where people dream more and are therefore more disappointed. The city was sitting there glowing, insistent, and smug, and I realised that I hated it yet, as fatigue overtook me and sleep beckoned, I just could not drag my eyes away.

21

He fell in love with the neon,

rolling on waves of heat.

A vivid blue

which burned his retinas,

turned his brain to mush.

Every generation is falling.

Hold on to your loved ones.

The present moment

lasts forever.

It dies

the second we do.

His fingers were stained

with black ink.

Did he see his reflection

in the darkened glass?

Was he aghast

at his beauty?

Father Time

will smite thy face

with wrinkles.

So in love with the neon!

Cool jazz whispers

through cheap tinny headphones.

Busy city syncopations,

Still he stared,

Elbows rested on the

back bedroom windowsill,

knelt down

as if in prayer.

London hovers

and seems to float in its valley,

shimmers,

writhes and tempts, and

all of those people

are under his command.

Do they look up at the distant wooded hills,

imagine him watching?

That neon,

a breath of ice in the summer.

Some cool for the psyche,

as vibrant as his imagination.

Words were never his friend,

though he'd spent the evening

trying to get them to dance across

the rough texture of a cheap notebook page

which soaked the ink and

ran one letter into the next.

Freeze neon cools all of his

metropolitan hopes,

nullifies his bravest moments

and fills his head

with meaning where there is none.

22

How can a soul sleep when a city just lingers, visible through the cracks in the threadbare curtains? How many people in that city of millions, at that moment, had trained a telescope on Grandmother's hill, and were peeping in through those curtains, and were watching me slumber on the bed? Grandmother was downstairs, asleep. And if I wanted to go to the toilet then I would have to go down the stairs and pass through all those rooms, opening and closing so many doors. It would take ages to navigate this brick warren, this cottage labyrinth.

I got out of bed and put on a t-shirt. I crept across the floor, even though I knew that Grandmother wouldn't be wearing her hearing aid and would not be able to hear a thing. The landing was small because there were only the two doors, and dark because there were no streetlights so deep in the woods. The stairs of the old cottage were steep and narrow, and they creaked alarmingly with every step. In the hallway, I paused for a while listening for any sound from the front room where Grandmother slept but could not hear a thing. Carefully, I unlatched the door to the middle room, closed it behind me as softly as I could, then crept across to the next door, which had once been the back door. The latches of this door were heavy, giant iron bolts which had to be slid out of their fittings. They'd been painted over so many times since they'd been installed that they had become stiff, and to do this quickly required concentration. Once this door was open, I descended the three flagstone steps into the kitchen, whose tiled floor was cold on the soles of my feet, and I realised that I should have worn some socks, because even in the middle of summer this part of the house felt very cold. The next door led to the small washing room, which was big enough just to have a wash basin, a medicine cupboard, and a stepladder leaned against the wall. I saw my reflection in the dark window, and I almost jumped. The next door, finally, led to the toilet.

I did what I had to do, then flushed. I started the return journey, washing my hands in the wash basin. But then I stopped for a little while, listening to the last of the water gurgling away into the ancient plumbing system. How many generations of my family, I wondered, had stood at this exact spot, looking out into the back garden so late at night? How many of them would never have realised what a privilege it was to be so absolutely quiet?

And that is when I realised how truly quiet it was. So quiet that it was almost heavy, a treacle-like quiet that my senses were trying to swim through and make sense of. No wonder my Grandad was meant to have had such good hearing. There had to be *something* to pin comprehension on, otherwise the slightest noise, the faintest sound, was going to be malevolent. I looked at my reflection and I felt that I could not bear much more of this if I were to romanticise the quietness of grandmother's house, because then I would never want to leave, and it would only magnify the noise of my everyday existence.

I put my nose to the glass of the window, and I tried to look out at the world, but there were no lights visible. You could not see the city from downstairs because Grandad's garage and shed and the various outbuildings were in the way. Anyone could have been out there, having wandered in from the woods, but who would be sneaking around in the woods in the middle of the night? The thought of it was spooky.

The scream came from nowhere. It shattered the silence, exploded the world. A cold scream, bloodcurdling and female, and in obvious distress. There was something inhuman about it, and yet at the same time incredibly human and primal, and I felt all my senses heighten. Was it Grandmother? No, it was too high-pitched. Who would be out there? What kind of disaster was occurring? My heart started beating, thumping in my ears. Maybe I'd imagined it, maybe I didn't hear it at all? My fingers were sweating as I gripped the cool ceramic of the wash basin. I thought of the police on the common in the fog, the body in the pond, the librarian with her medical episode. Had I become immune to the calamities of other people? Or was I attracting them, was fortune putting me in places where I was a witness to terrible things?

I did not want to be a witness. The scream had been so piercing. I did not want any part of this, at least, not at that moment, because I did not know enough about the world. I didn't know how I was supposed to react. The scream had shattered everything, and I wanted to go back to my bed. Whatever bad there was in the world could not penetrate the fortress of my grandmother's house so long as all the doors remained shut and bolted. As quickly as I could, I retraced my steps, locking and bolting all the doors behind me, and I went back up the narrow creaky stairs to the back bedroom with its view of the uncaring city, and I got into bed, and I pulled the covers over my head.

23

Dizzy.

I could not sleep.

Or was I merely dreaming

That I could not sleep?

24

How can any of this be true? I would be ill a lot in those days. I'd pick up any virus that came along, and some of these would only last for a few hours, or even just for the night. I had started feeling a little bit off-colour as the evening had drawn in, though Grandmother had gone to bed early, and I'd pretended that I would be doing the same yet knowing that I had a few good hours left in me, and some bad ones, too. It became a ritual, whether I was feeling good or not. Midnight would come and go as if it meant nothing. Tonight, though, my head - on account of the virus or whatever it was – and the scream, of course – hearing that scream - felt as if it were on fire, and it seemed a shame to waste these precious hours stolen from the night, but I went to bed, too. I mean, I tried to sleep, in that back bedroom with its view out over London, as Grandmother slept downstairs, and the motorway was roaring.

And I couldn't stop thinking about moths, because there were lots of moths in Grandmother's house after dark, and they'd flit around the lampshades like satellites around the planet, but more erratically, as if each moment they were racked with indecision, and I hated that the moth's whole time was spent changing their minds every second, every fraction of a second, and how exhausting that must have been for them and for the other moths. And as I thought about the moths, and what it must have been like to be a moth, I could feel the sheets of the bed getting soaked with my own sweat, and my hair was wet, and I became a moth for a few seconds buzzing around the lampshade in my room, buzzing and fluttering until I realised with a sense of relief that the light wasn't even turned on, and that I was still a human after all.

When Grandmother made tea, she would spoon tea leaves into the teapot and she would say, 'One for each person, and one for the pot'. I must have picked up the virus from her, the fever, or whatever it was, or perhaps it was her cooking and something that I'd eaten, or perhaps it was an allergic reaction to the mould and the damp, or perhaps it was because it was so tiring carrying those powdery folded wings around all the time, magnificently natural for the soul, powdered wings trailing behind unfurled for the light. I wake again, once more relieved that I am not a moth, and I sit up in the bed and I look at the lights of London, and even I am attracted to those lights, that neon, those illuminated street signs, the same way that a moth might be.

Soaked sheets. Soaked pillow. Wasn't this my mother's room when she was a kid? How did she get on with the moths? Perhaps Grandmother picked up the virus from one of her friends at the day care centre. Carried it without realising that she was infected. Or did an excellent job of making it look like everything was okay. What time was it? I did not want to lie down on those bedclothes anymore, so I sat on the edge of the bed, and I looked at the lights of the capital down there. If I unfocused my eyes they looked like sodium stars in a nonsensical constellation. But wasn't the universe itself nonsensical? I put up a hand and I blotted out the whole of the East End. Did anyone down there even realise that I'd just blotted them from existence? Surely, I was now the most important person in the world, or perhaps I was the most insignificant. If I were the most insignificant person in the world, then that would make me more significant, wouldn't it? Thereby nullifying any insignificance. Where did the moths flit in a time before fire? I was going round in circles.

One for each person and one for the pot.

The bed sheets were still damp, and I didn't want to lie down on them, so I got up for a bit and I stood at the back

69

bedroom window. The rain sounded gentle as if it was pretending that it wasn't there. I looked at my Grandfather's workshop down at the bottom of the garden and I thought how cosy it must have been to tinker in there while it was raining, listening to the sound of the rain on the corrugated iron roof, while he busied himself with something intricate at his work bench involving sharp tools, accurate calculations, focus, the glare from the spotlight, precise measurements, unbelievable patience. If only I could be so patient and so well-crafted. If only I could go into his workshop, just for a bit.

What was stopping me? Well, the rain, for a start. The fever. Grandmother asleep downstairs. All those doors that you must pass through. And the fact that I was not the sort of person who would, necessarily, I don't, what I'm trying to say is, we're built differently, my grandfather and I, configured differently, and to go there would have been to somehow . . . Cheapen his work, because I had a soul which seemed incapable of . . . The key to the workshop was hung on a hook by the back door, but even so, it would have been wrong, wouldn't it? Grandfather was gone now, he would have no knowledge of my going in there, and hardly anyone else has been in there since he died, but it would have been wrong, wouldn't it? I wouldn't want to wake Grandmother, or worse, be caught sneaking out, thereby leading to an awkward conversation in which I'd have to explain what I was going to do, and she would not have been able to understand why someone configured so differently to Grandfather would be wanting to go down there at all, because for her the existence of the workshop at the bottom of the garden was entirely normal and not at all magical. Or she might even have understood that there was an inherent romance about a midnight expedition to Grandfather's shed and she might even have put the kettle on for my eventual return, one for each person and one for the pot.

I told myself that the idea was stupid, and I sat down again on the bed, and the I felt a little bit dissociated from the world around me, which must have been because of the virus. I felt hot all over, and then I felt immediately cold, and I put my hand to my head and my hair was soaking wet, and I started thinking about moths again and how the moths might flit around *me*, attracted by the heat and the damp, until I remembered that it's light that moths are attracted to, that I must have been very tired because I'd got it all wrong, but the workshop was there and I might never get another chance to go and see it on my own at midnight and have a look inside, because it felt like the night was already special.

The energy came from nowhere. I found a t-shirt and pulled on some shorts, some trainers, and opened the old-fashioned bedroom door latch ever so quietly and almost floated down the steep stairs. Every movement seemed conducted ahead of myself, as if my consciousness were left behind, several seconds behind, lagging behind my physicality. I was halfway down the stairs before I'd decided whether it was worth getting off the bed. The t-shirt absorbed some of the sweat. When my mother was a girl, did she ever envisage that one day her son would be walking down this very same narrow, steep staircase of this two-up two-down worker's cottage on a hill surrounded by forest, in the middle of the night, the lights of London in the distance shining so bright? My legs felt like jelly, and this made me nervous. No moths a-swirl. I was on my own, and it really did feel like it.

Hallway, back room, kitchen. The doors were all opened with a creak shut and then locked and latched, the handles and bolts cool to my touch. I didn't hear a sound from Grandmother asleep in the front room. My sweaty palms slipped, and the kitchen door latch clacked unnecessarily, and this made me sweat even more. I could just make it all out in the dark because there were no streetlights out here in the woods, no moon, no sign at all that any of these rooms had windows. How on earth had I managed to get this far without seeing anything? I was still moments ahead of myself, that is how. It's like I had a new super-power. How jealous people would be! I had to wipe the sweat from my eyes as I reached for the key, that massive iron key hung on the hook next to the back door. I had to wipe the stinging sweat away, and wipe the doubt away, I had to imbue the moment with some mystique because this was Grandfather's key. The mystique was drowned amid the fever and the heat and the dark, and the key was like a ceremonial key like I'd won the freedom of a small city somewhere, because of my new super-power of being moments ahead of myself, and the moths beat their powdery wings in a sarcastic applause.

The rain felt like cold needles. The night, though, was muggy. A slight breeze froze the sweat clinging to my body. I set off away from the back door and down the long back lawn. *Daniel, Daniel, what are you doing?* Sixty-eight steps from Grandfather's workshop. The key tasted metallic through my fingers. The rain smelled red. I was now further from myself than I had ever been - I was still halfway down the stairs, trying not to make them creak so as to not wake Grandmother, while here was my body now three quarters of the way down the long back lawn and the apple tree which had incredibly small and bitter apples, which Grandmother had tried to sell to a door-to-door fruit vendor, and he'd tasted one and said no, and then she had charged him 30p for the apple that he had tasted. And now I was at the bottom of the garden under the neighbour's overhanging oak tree where the ground was ankle-deep in leaves and mulch, and it was piled up around the bottom of the workshop door because nobody had opened the door for months. And those apples were so bitter, and the key was like a ceremonial key that comes with the freedom of the city, and the moths were beating

their powdery wings in sarcastic applause, and the key went in
the lock first time, and the mechanism worked so smoothly, and I
was ankle deep in cold wet leaves and yet I was still only three
quarters of the way down the stairs.

Not long after they married,

my grandfather built a tin shack workshop

away from the house,

whose corrugated roof

speckled tinny with scratchy rain

like the soundtrack

of an old black and white film.

Inside, he would tinker, operating

lathes and drills and keeping

screws and bolts in carefully labelled drawers,

a spotlight illuminating his workbench,

the paraphernalia of invention.

And I would watch him work,

mesmerised by the careful choreography

of mechanised hardware,

dangerous belts,

curls of shaved metal,

the cacophony of creation,

how exact he invariably was.

Daniel, Daniel, what are you doing? Daniel Cooper?

The bed was too damp to sleep on.

The shack was smaller, because I was taller, now. I was higher up. And it looked so tiny in there, so dark and cramped and there weren't any of the gaps between the various machines that I'd remembered from when I was younger, and it all seemed crammed in, and I turned the light on and the light was dull and no matter how hard I tried, I couldn't imagine my grandfather working there. I never once towered over him. I never once was taller than he was. And it was all so . . . so old and . . . dusty and . . . there were cobwebs, and the tins he put things in were rusty and . . . the floor was just bare earth packed down, and the curtains were scraps of material which were dirty and faded and . . . it's not like time had moved on, it's just that . . . I had no concept of untidiness or filth the times I stood there watching him working his lathe and his drill, and he must have felt so cosy nonetheless, for I was too young to have any idea that sometimes adults liked to play, too.

A world apart from the rest of the house, beyond the lawn which he'd cut with a scythe, beyond the apple tree with its sour fruit, underneath the limbs of the neighbour's oak, acorns falling on the corrugated iron roof, *donk donk donk*.

I floated on feather legs above the cold packed earth floor. Grandfather had never let me in this far. The tools were exactly where he left them the last time he worked at his bench. It looked like a museum exhibit. The windows looked out past and through the hedge at the lights of the city. I floated over everything, hardly daring to touch. Brushes in a jam jar soaking in thinners that had long since evaporated. Moths circle the light, and I try to bat them away.

'You're floating', Tina says.

She was in the doorway. She took me by surprise, and I floated back down to the floor of the workshop.

'I . . I . .'.

The glow from the low watt bulb illuminated each individual sequin stitched onto her dress.

'Yes?'

'I was just looking'.

'Honey, you don't have to explain to me'.

'I thought I'd come down and see if it jogged any memories'.

'And to have yourself a little adventure?'

She opened her tiny clutch bag and took out a lipstick and a mirror. She made lip shapes like a goldfish as she put on her make-up.

'Sort of'.

'Well then, looks like the two of us are going to have this adventure together'.

'That's not what I would call it'.

'Babes . .'. She screwed the base of her lipstick, snapped the mirror shut, placed them back in her handbag. 'Every moment with me is an adventure. Look', she said, pointing.

A fox was snuffling around the pile of leaves piled up at the base of the door.

I gasped.

'I've seen foxes before', I said, though I was taken aback by the brazenness of the fox, the way that it went about its business as if neither of us were there.

'This place is filthy, sweetheart'. She leaned inside and ran a gloved finger along the work bench. 'Absolutely filthy'.

'It was Grandad's shed'.

'It could do with a good clean'.

'So could you'.

It wasn't the most intelligent of comments, but it was late at night, and I wasn't feeling too good.

'I hope you're being careful around those machines'.

'I am!'

She bent down a little as she entered the workshop so that her beehive hairstyle didn't touch the doorframe. She was wearing her sculpted blond wig with the big bow in it, and there was just about enough clearance with the doorframe. There was a slight look of disgust on her face.

'You wouldn't want to get your feather boa caught on some of those gears and cogs', she said, looking at the lathe.

'I don't wear feather boas. Only you wear feather boas.'

'Honey, I'm known for my style'.

'You're an embarrassment'.

We watched the moths, for a while. They circled the small light which Grandfather had screwed to one of the wooden beams of the workshop roof. Some of the moths went clockwise around the lightbulb, some went anticlockwise, some didn't even seem to have a plan, they just advanced on it, then backed away, then came back, and it was all very confusing.

There was heat emanating from the fox, rippling the air around it which crackled and fizzed.

'Why do you have to be so embarrassing?'

'Just look at the state of that box of lug-nuts'.

Heat rose up from the fox as it snuffled and pawed the ground. I was worried that it would set fire to the dead leaves, the shed, the night.

'Grandad would never have wanted someone like you in here'.

'For the sake of your safety, no doubt'.

'No, I mean . . '.

Moths around the light. The flame-vixen sizzling. Acorns on the corrugated iron roof. The sour apple tree. *One for each person and one for the pot.* I was three quarters of the way down the stairs, now. The lights of London just hanging there, visible beyond the tattered rag curtains of Grandad's workshop shack windows.

'Then why else wouldn't he want me in here?', Tina asked.

'Because .. He would have been . . . He would have been disgusted'.

'He would have been amused but not disgusted. He would have been very civil. Your Grandfather was a gentleman'.

'He would have been disgusted'.

'Follow me', the fox said.

'You can't hide forever', Tina said.

'Follow me'.

The air around the animal was distorted, waving and crackling.

'We'd better do what she says'.

'She?'

'She's a vixen. She owns the night. Or at the very least, *this* night'.

'I'm so hot', I said, as I turned off the workshop light, stepped out, pushed the door closed. I turned the giant key in the lock, like Grandfather must have done thousands of times. 'My t-shirt is soaked in sweat'.

'Follow me'.

I remember when I was a kid, and Grandfather was talking about the foxes in the woods, and I was only young and I'd said to him that I wanted to have a fox as a pet, and he'd said that he had a plan to get one, all you needed was a house brick and some pepper, and you put the house brick on the ground and you sprinkled pepper on it, and the fox came along and thought, *oh, what's this?*, and it bent down and sniffed the house brick and the pepper went up its nose, and it sneezed, and it hit its head on the brick, and it knocked itself out cold, and hey presto, you've got yourself a fox.

But this fox was too authoritative for such shenanigans.

The vixen was trotting now across the back lawn, past the apple tree and up to the house. I almost had to run to keep up. Tina trod awkwardly in her heels on the soft rain-soaked lawn. We must have looked so weird, the three of us. From the back, the house, with all its additions and extensions, looked like a jumble of red bricks, cubes and rectangles and windows and the slate tile roof glistened in the drizzle. I felt weak and easily led. I wondered if we were going to go back inside, which could have been weird because I was now almost down the stairs and that meant that I would meet me and I shuddered to think what might happen, but we went past the back door and down the side next to the hedge, and then out into the small front garden, and then, without even looking, the vixen was across the road and into the woods.

'Not so fast!', Tina said. She was having to lift the hem of her red sequin dress so that she could take bigger strides and run faster.

'I think I've lost the fox'.

'Follow her! And be careful of the road'.

I looked both ways. There was nothing coming, and Tina had caught up. We crossed together and crashed through the bracken at the edge of the wood, and then I caught a glimpse of the vixen again, shimmering the air around her as she did so. And once she knew that we were within range, she set off again.

'Not far now!', she said.

We clambered up the steep hill following the fox. I looked back at Tina in the murk and the gloom, and her face betrayed a certain revulsion, for she was trying her best not to get her shoes or her dress muddy or too wet. The vixen waited for us at the top of the hill. I stumbled on the roots of a tree, and she told me to be careful, but we were almost there, she said, very nearly there. At the top of the hill, the view through the trees of nighttime London in its valley was spectacular, but I had no time to stop because now the fox was bolting down the hill in a direction I'd never been before. The descent was particularly hazardous for Tina, and we had to wait for her, and once she'd caught up, we waited a little and then were off again.

At the bottom of the hill, we came on a narrow lane. Unmade, it consisted of two parallel tracks with a ridge of grass in the centre. We stopped on the side of this track, which led off into the darkness on either side, and Tina told me to wait.

'But there's obviously no traffic', I pointed out.

'Just wait'.

The glow off the heat-vixen sizzled the air as it stood in the middle of the track.

'Listen', Tina said.

'I can't hear anything'.

'Just listen!'

There was a rhythm to the night. Why hadn't I noticed it before? The sound of an engine, rattling and clanking further along the lane. A vehicle was coming, but it did not sound like a car. It didn't sound modern. This made me on edge, but I did not know why. It seemed inconceivable that this narrow lane could accommodate anything wider than a normal car. It sounded big.

80

The sound of it kept getting quieter as if wound its way along the track, and then the clattering became more pronounced. It was getting closer.

'I'm scared', I whispered.

The heart-vixen was still sitting in the middle of the track. It looked in the direction that the noise was coming from. It, too, could sense its approach. At last, the trees in the distance were lit by a beam of light, which wavered and bounced as the vehicle's basic suspension negotiated the potholes of the woodland track. And then the headlights of the vehicle came into view as it rounded a corner. I had to put a hand up in front of my eyes to shield them from the glare. The clattering and chugging of the engine became louder as it neared us, and I felt an impulse to turn and run. Tina's sequin dress sparkled iridescent in the beam from the headlights. The heart-vixen stood on all fours as if to greet the machine, though I was afraid that it would not stop and would injure the fox. It was all too much. It was all too wearying, as my emotions attempted to navigate the night's indistinctness. Clatter, clatter, clatter. At last, with a squeal from its ineffectual brakes, the contraption came to a halt a few yards away, its engine ticking over, until its operator switched off the engine and the lights and the thing just sat there in the gloom, all spiky metal and wheels and glass.

Darkness. I could not see anything.

'Who is it?', I asked.

'I'll find out', Tina said.

'No! Don't!'

My eyes started to adjust to the gloom. I could see the mudguards and radiator of an old charabanc in the darkness, but I could not see who the driver was. He was wearing a hat and goggles. He was a young man, and he sat on the driver's seat behind the large steering wheel, ever so patiently, with his hands on his lap.

'I think he's waiting', Tina said.

'Don't go', I whispered.

'Honey! Don't you recognise him? He's your Grandfather'.

'But..'.

I looked closer at the young man in the wax jacket and the goggles. The young man, sitting there so patiently behind the wheel, the same way that Grandad used to sit in his Triumph Herald while waiting for Grandmother to come out from the supermarket. I wanted to go and see him. I wanted him to be my Grandfather, but I knew that it was impossible. It could not be him. The young man sitting there, staring into space, that could not be him. And the old vehicle, the old charabanc with its high chassis and its rows of open-top empty seats, when had Grandad ever driven one of those? The answer was simple, of course. Before I came along. He had a whole life which he'd almost lived to the full before I came along. Before I came along. The world did not revolve around me.

'But he's younger'.

'Yes, he is'.

'And he's . . . Dead'.

'I shall go and speak with him', Tina said.

'OK'.

Because it could not have been him, of course. And I was afraid that the night might fold in on itself. Tina stepped on to the track and approached the old charabanc. The driver turned his head to speak to her as she got near to the door. She put one high-heeled shoe on the running board. It was weird seeing Tina chatting with the younger version of my dead grandfather, like two parts of my life meeting for the first time. I could not hear any actual words, but I could see them chatting, and I saw the young man pass some material to Tina, which she took in her gloved hand. She then walked back up the track towards me.

'He says you were right not to speak to him'.

'Who was it?'

'Your Grandfather. I told you he was your Grandfather'.

'What is he doing here?'

'He's come to see it'.

'To see what?'

'The Neon Yak, of course'.

'The Neon Yak is coming?!'

'Yes. Your Grandfather has come all this way to make sure of one thing'.

'And what's that?'

'He wants to make sure that you don't see it'.

'I want to see it!'

'He says that it wouldn't be right'.

'It will be right! What does he know? I want to see it, you know that I want to see it, why doesn't he want me to see it?'

I felt so hot.

'He says that it might not even be the Neon Yak. It might be an ibex, or a zebu. Such things have been known to occur. Fortune has its own sense of playfulness, you know?'

'Grandad had time to tell you all this?'

'So, he has given me an item and he says you must wear it'.

Tina held out the object that my Grandfather had given her. It was a scarf. It was a blindfold.

'This doesn't make sense', I said. 'Why bring me all the way out here just to make sure I purposefully miss seeing the one thing that I have always wanted to see?'

'But have you always wanted to see it?'

'Yes!'

'I'm not sure you've thought this through'.

'You know it's true!'

Tina looked right at me, and she put her hands on my shoulders.

'Grandad knows what you want', she whispered. 'He knows who you are. He knows you as a person. He understands the whole situation in a much wider context. And he says that you must wear the blindfold'.

I put the blindfold over my face and over my eyes and I tied it at the back. I was still at the bottom of the stairs, or was I now halfway down? I was in the woods, and I could hear the foliage rustling, I could hear Tina's dress rustling, I could hear the rain on the leaves and the usual suburban sounds. And then, oh, I sensed it. A glow, which came through the fabric of the blindfold. Oh, I sensed it. I could taste the air. The glow was white, or was it blue, or was it pink? Feint at first, it grew bigger, more intense, and sizzled the night. I could hear the rhythmic tread of hooves heavy on the peaty earth. I could hear a growling sound, a snuffling sound, the noise of a beast. And the glow, oh, it was so bright that I could feel the heat of it. It glowed brighter and brighter. 'Don't move', Tina said, 'Just don't move'. It was so bright that I had to clamp my eyes shut. I could feel a waft of air from its nose, its breath on my face, for it was right there in front of me, its nose was inches from the end of my own, it sniffed, and sniffed, and sniffed again, and it grunted, and then it was gone, it had turned away and it was gone off into the undergrowth, it was gone.

'Oh, sweetheart', Tina said.

'Tina .. Grandad . .'.

'Oh sweetheart, it was beautiful', she said.

And then came the silence. The silence was the most uncomfortable part. The most unfathomable part. Where had everyone gone? Where had the suburbs gone, where had existence gone? Why could I only hear the road of blood in my ears? I'd felt the Neon Yak's hot breath on my face, clammy and pungent, but now it was quiet, and I could imagine the moths flitting to the glow from its electric flanks, and I was sad because I had wanted to see it, and I was conscious that perhaps they were right, perhaps Tina and my Grandfather were right because I didn't want to see it yet, I wasn't ready. I didn't want to enter a world and pretend to be someone I wasn't, or, no, hang on, wasn't this what I was already doing? I slid the blindfold off. Grandfather's charabanc was gone, and we were just standing in the middle of the woods.

'You haven't changed', I said.

'It wasn't meant for me'.

'But you saw it, didn't you?'

'It wasn't meant for me'.

I couldn't understand. She was still Tina. She hadn't changed into a man, and her voice hadn't become deeper or less feminine.

'Did you close your eyes?'

'Change only comes', she said, 'If you want it'.

'So you want to be the way you are?'

'I don't want to be who I am. I am the way I am'.

'But . .'.

 I really couldn't understand her way of thinking.

'I don't feel well', I said.

The lane was gone. The old car, too. It was as if nothing had happened. No flame-vixen, no Grandfather.

I was at the bottom of the stairs; my wet fingers cling on to the doorframe.

'You're burning up', Tina said.

'Like the flame-vixen'.

'You're soaking wet'.

'It's the rain', I lied.

'Sweetheart, we have to get you inside'.

I did not want to move, because I was hot, and I was cold. I could feel my damp t-shirt sticking to my back and this made me shiver. The sweat was rolling down my forehead into my eyes. I could feel the clammy root of the tree on the back of my legs.

'I think I'm going to faint'.

'Oh, honey'.

I got up. The world felt very unsteady. I felt as if the moths were circling around me, but there was nothing. Or maybe I was circling around them. I could not really work out what was happening. The floor was coming up at me, but then it went away again.

'How did it happen?', I asked.

'You have obviously got some sort of fever. You will have to sleep it off'.

'I mean - the moths, the bats, the fox .. '.

'Darling, I wouldn't want to spoil the magic'.

'Was it an illusion?'

'Yes, dear, it probably was'.

I stumbled a bit and put a hand flat on the horny bark of a tree trunk. I felt it coarse under my fingers. Or was it the doorframe in the hall at the bottom of the stairs?

'Sometimes', Tina was saying, 'it's best to preserve the mystique'.

'There's no time for mystique when you're not feeling too well', I told her.

It was a long way back to Grandmother's house, and my head was full of moths and bats. We emerged from the woodland at the tarmac road. There were no cars, which is just as well, because everything else was now dancing. Grandmother's cottage sat small and embarrassed on the other side of the road. One window upstairs, one window downstairs. It could not be so small, was it shrinking? Was I now trapped inside? The outside didn't look big enough to contain the inside.

'You need to get to bed', Tina said.

'I don't want to'.

'It's probably something you've eaten'.

'I won't be able to sleep', I told her.

I did not want to tell her that I could feel myself changing inside. That's what was happening. It was like the world had suddenly decided to give me some more experience of living. I cannot really explain it, not even now, not even with the benefit of several years. Or had my brain had turned against me, decided that I was being foolish because I was getting older, and I was trying to discount the magic? There was a different version of myself. Except there was, wasn't there? Standing at the bottom of the stairs.

Through the back door as quietly as I could. Tina had vanished, like she always seemed to do when my mind was occupied with something else. I closed the back door, passed through the kitchen, the room at the rear, opened the hallway and almost jumped out of my skin to see me there.

'You're all wet', I said.

'So are you', I said.

'Where have you been?', I said.

'Here all the time', I said.

And we merged after that, and then I sat on the bottom step of the stairs. Had it really taken so long to clamber down? Wearily, warily, I got up, and I could feel the fever lifting if only a little. I opened the door to the back room and sat on the chair in front of the television, and I turned it on.

Grandmother's television was old, and it took a while to warm up, the tiny dot in the middle getting larger and larger, and then the picture appeared. I turned the volume down, but the room was filled with that high-pitched whine, and the picture flickered and sent flickers throughout the back room and both the whine, and the flickering made me feel ill. I closed my eyes, and I tried not to faint. When I opened them, the picture on the screen was of some action film or television film. There was a gunfight going on, in the stairwell of the CN Tower in Toronto. Two men were firing at each other from one landing to the next, but they kept missing. One of them was wearing a suit. This was obviously the big finale of the film, or the television show and the stand-off was carefully choreographed. I concentrated on the image on the screen, and I started to feel a little better. One of them would have to get shot, eventually. I could also feel a breeze. Tina was fanning me. Tina was fanning me with Grandmother's newspaper. Waft, waft, waft. She was fanning, fanning.

'Have you just had a nightmare?', she asked.

Her sequin dress reflected the television screen hundreds, thousands of times.

Waft, waft, waft.

'I don't know', I replied.

89

I could feel something lumpy and hard in the pocket of my shorts. I put my hand in and tried to feel it with my fingers? What was it? Metal, and warm, and slightly curved. I pulled it out of the pocket a little bit and saw that it was the key to Grandfather's workshop, wrapped in the blindfold.

'I think . . . I think . . '.

But I couldn't.

25

The police on the common, the body in the pond, the fight on the street, the scream in the dark, the bats, the moths, the Neon Yak, the background rumble of traffic on the motorway, the whole of London just sitting there, how could I sleep?

But I was asleep within seconds.

And when I woke, I was feeling much, much better.

26

Grandmother explained that the sound I'd heard had been a vixen. The noise of their piercing scream, she told me, is uncannily human.

27

Once upon a dark forest,

in whose ferny depths

mysterious night-time rustling and

the crack whip snap of pigeon wings

primed a soul for the desolate,

there was a marked

fairy-tale acceptance of the banal.

Misty cling rain would glisten on a slate tile roof,

fish-scale overlaps in the deep deep woods,

a two-up two-down cottage in whose

various outbuildings,

long-since reclaimed by the wild forest,

hinted at the slow advance and the retreat

of a city which long ago

decided to look elsewhere,

to leave behind a tide of forgetting,

cold rooms, a popping gas fire,

and furniture from three generations back.

There was no appetite for ambition

beyond the immediacy of comfort

and stretches of silence almost Zen,

were it not for the murmur of the unspoken,

traffic rumbles, aircraft whines,

a son-in-law's brother whose overcoat

smelled of city districts and different boroughs,

the hum of a fridge,

cars on the wet road.

And no-one ever spoke of frightening things.

the woods were free of wolves and ogres too,

and so long as it were kept at an arm's length,

the city could never overspill its suburban boundaries,

tempt one into dreaming, for no-one has the right

to make their mark but a fool.

The gas fire popped with certainty, and it was all

once upon a dark forest.

3

28

It was so noisy when I got back home. Like the place itself was punishing me for having been elsewhere. Had word got around that I had been hiding from real life, did the world now want to prove to me that it was still there? The kids next door were screaming for no reason, crashing around in their shared bedroom which was right next to mine. At one moment they started slapping the wall, slap slap slap slap slap. Had someone told them to do this, or did they just decide on their own? Downstairs, their parents played loud music which throbbed the floorboards. Vom vom vom vom vom. Slap slap slap slap slap. Scream.

'Just go round', Tina said, 'and tell them to be quiet'.

'I can't. They'll be very annoyed. They'll punch me'.

'Be a man'.

'You're a fine one to talk'.

Were all planets this noisy?

The sun and the heat had come back, now that I was home. The world smelled again of creosote and tarmac, aviation fuel, motorway exhaust. There was shouting in the street -why couldn't people just have normal conversations? - and revving engines, boy racers, screeching tyres. The roundabout with its *Mister Scott is a Tosser* motif was melting in the heat. The Pyromaniac had his shirt off, which was not as appealing as when Luke had taken his shirt off, not that I should have been looking at such because my heterosexuality still had not kicked in. The Pyromaniac's milky white skin constructed against the green of the privet hedge as he set fire to a cardboard box and stood back to admire his work.

'How do you keep so cool?', I asked Tina.

'Honey, I don't need to keep cool. I *am* cool'.

'No, but seriously'.

'Think about it, Twinkle Toes. I keep cool because I don't exist'.

I had forgotten.

29

I crouched down, almost crawled, and entered the thicket. Entangled rhododendron branches barred my way and added their natural confusion to the morning. It felt cooler in there, a world shaded from the hot sun. Keep going, Danny, you jungle explorer, miles in the middle of nowhere, perhaps. Can you hear the sparrows, the crows, the pigeons? The planes? Better than the usual noise. Soon I will be in my private place.

I came out into bright sunshine, so bright it hurt my eyes for a second or two. And there was that patch of long grass that nobody else knew about. Butterflies fluttered their wings, white butterflies vivid and the same colour as the Pyromaniac with his shirt off. Bees buzzed. You could smell the pollen and the sweetness from the purple flowers of the rhododendrons. You could smell the sap in the trees.

I sat down in the long grass, cross-legged. The grass tickled my bare legs. I looked at the ground and the dried dirt in between the blades of grass, and I could see ants. They looked so busy, moving punctuation in sentences of oblivion, they obviously had so much to do. I had books to read, and I had my notebook with me in case I felt like doing some writing. I could be here all day; it was either this or the library.

One thing that I was always worried about when I was in my private place was that I could get disoriented and forget which rhododendron bush it was that I had emerged from, because if you weren't concentrating then they all looked the same, and that when it was time to go home I'd enter the wrong thicket and get hopelessly lost, which would be very embarrassing, but the way home was imprinted on my memory because I hated going there so much.

I wondered what it was like here before they built the suburbs. The housing estate was only a mile away, you could walk there in less than half an hour. Was the ground they built the 'estate' on just like this? All vegetation and shrubbery, trees, private places?

In a couple of weeks, I would be at school. Proper secondary school, which looked from the outside very much like a factory with its rows and rows of windows and its tower block. It looked like a small town behind its fence. As a special treat before that, though, my uncle had invited me along for a week to Scout camp somewhere in the mountains. I wasn't in the Scouts, but Uncle was a Scout leader in a different town and for some reason they thought I should go along and join them and do all the masculine things that the Scouts were meant to do. Perhaps it might do me some good. Perhaps the heterosexuality would finally kick in if I was surrounded by tents and tents of boisterous boys. I didn't really want to go, but I felt bad even deciding this. I wasn't yet ready to become another person. At least, I told myself, I would be away from the noise.

An ant crawled over my leg. I brushed it off.

I knew, though, that things were changing. I hadn't even seen the Neon Yak, and things were changing. I *would* become another person, no matter what happened. I would soon be at secondary school. I'd have to catch a bus every morning to that place, right there near to the airport. It would be so loud, and even though I loved aircraft, it seemed a shame that I would be so near to them and yet so incapable of enjoying the experience. And I'd have my first girlfriend and experience all kinds of emotions attached to this. I'd find someone with long hair and a friendly smile, and she would be everything that I'd ever wanted, and it would all just slot into place and I really would not miss the person that I was right at this moment. I would tell her about Tina, and she would just laugh.

I lay back in the grass. I looked up at the perfect blue sky. It was so blue that I'd never seen another blue like it, not even the blue of the motorway signs that I had seen from Grandmother's back bedroom window. I wondered what would happen if I levitated right at this moment. There would be no ceiling to save me this time, I'd just go floating up and up and people would say, *hey, you will never guess what happened to Danny Cooper, up, up he went!* And then I'd never have to worry about changing, or seeing the Neon Yak, because that's the sort of person that I would be.

I stopped daydreaming and I sat up. I brushed the ants from my t-shirt and legs. There was a line of them making their way to a discarded chocolate bar wrapper.

A discarded chocolate bar wrapper.

The sudden realisation hit me. I'd half-noticed the chocolate bar wrapper, but I hadn't really thought about it. I was so accustomed to litter, living on the 'estate'. A discarded chocolate bar wrapper meant that someone else had been here, because I'd never sat here and eaten a chocolate bar, and if I had, then I certainly would not have left litter. Which meant that other people came here. Which meant that only a certain percentage of these were the sort to leave litter. Which meant that I was never truly on my own. Which meant - which meant - that this was not *my* Private Place.

I got up at once. I looked around but could hear nothing beyond grasshoppers, pigeons, sparrows, buzzing. Other people had been here! And really, it should not have come as a surprise, because there were so many people living in the suburbs and there were millions living in the city that surely it was not just me who had discovered this place and who came here. I would have to share it. Because - and oh, this thought should have come as a comfort even though it was annoying - because there were others like me. I was not unique.

30

I hardly saw the mountains because they hid behind waves of mist which would occasionally lift and reveal stark rock faces, waterfalls, bleak views in a grey world, for the drizzle was persistent. A farmer had allowed us use of his fields, which lay down in a hollow where a river, wide and stony, narrowed down to a right-angle turn. The other side of the river was dense woodland, impenetrable, ragged, and clinging on to the foothills of an unseen mountain.

We had pitched out tents on the inside of the riverbank, which was the only flat part of the field that we had been allocated. The older Scouts looked very grown-up and were loud and had deep voices, but they knew their way around a tent and got things done without too much fuss. The younger Scouts were my age, though we did not mix much, and I had nothing in common with them. I had my own tent, while they had to share. They saw me as my uncle's pet. Uncle had to help me put up my tent.

We were two hundred and fifty miles from home, and I was looking forward to the silence, but Uncle seemed to want to include me in all the Scout's activities. A hastily arranged game of rounders came undone because the field was too steep, and after half a day, the grass was starting to become a muddy quagmire. We all wore our waterproof clothing the whole time, which was uncomfortable even for the older Scouts, of whom there were a couple more due to arrive that first evening.

'Honey, I'm booking into a hotel', Tina would have said.

'Thanks. Just desert me, I don't care'.

'I'm not built for this'.

My tent had a sleeping bag and just about enough room for my backpack. The rain made a noise very much like the scratchy soundtrack of an old black and white film. It felt like the sort of place where I might be very cosy. Perhaps when the heterosexuality kicked in, I'd be able to bring my first girlfriend back here, but I had not even seen the Neon Yak, its electric flanks reflected on the river surface.

Uncle and the scout leaders put up a marquee under which we could have our meals seated at wooden benches, and it was here that I was gathered with the others when the older scouts turned up. I recognised Luke at once, and my heart did a strange little flip of recognition. Grinning, smiling, floppy-fringed and exuberant, he acted as though everything was perfectly normal, but he did not even look my way, and once he and the others were off, putting up their tents, Uncle started speaking to us all in hushed tones.

'Now listen. We are all going to have to be very nice to him because something awful has happened recently to his family.'

And he left it at that, and would not answer any questions, but I knew exactly what it was that he was referring to.

Birds sang in the evening as the sun set behind the mountains. There was no traffic noise here, no aircraft, no music, nothing beyond the continual tinkling sound that the river made as it bounced over rocks and boulders. Everything smelled damp and musty, not least myself, wrapped up in a waterproof jacket all day, yet I was somehow glad because it was a smell I associated with manliness. Not for me the comforts of home! But I could read my books once the sun had gone down, using a torch which took big batteries, and the shouting and the playfulness and the silliness of the younger scouts, with their voices echoing back from the hills around us, reminded me of evenings on the 'estate'. I understood that there was no ill-intent behind the shouting and that it was conducted to show the joy they felt in each other's company and their inherent manliness, and yet I wondered why it was that they seemed intent to impose their personality on the surrounding environment. I reasoned, people are simply happy being alive, and that this was also true back home, with the kids next door and the music and the Pyromaniac. And if that was the case, then why didn't I ever want to join in and do the same?

31

'Honey, I walked into the village. You should have seen them stare!'

'I'm not surprised'.

'They obviously had never seen a proper lady'.

'And they haven't seen a proper lady'.

'Sweetie-Pie. This is serious. There. Is. No. Off licence'.

'Shocking. We're in the middle of the Welsh mountains'.

'I went to the pub, and I belted out some Judy Garland. Those grizzled old farmers did not know what had hit them'.

'You're disgusting'.

'But they loved every minute, honey. They wanted more. And you know the golden rule of show business, love. Always leave them wanting more'.

'You're so embarrassing'.

'Is that why you keep me hidden away? So that Luke does not see me?'

'What's that meant to mean?'

'Honey, I'm going rock-climbing. I've decided. I want to be the first drag queen to climb up the mountain'.

'Go for it'.

'You could sound more enthusiastic'.

'Go for it!'

'In my finest ruby red sequin dress. The backless one I wore that second day we stayed with your grandmother'.

'Nothing's stopping you'.

'And I'm going to get to the top, sweetie pie. And everyone will be so amazed'.

'They might whisk you away to Hollywood. And then I will never have to see you again'.

'Darling, I'm with you for life'.

32

The Scouts my age meant nothing to me, for they were uniform in their waterproof macs and wellington boots, and they said nothing of any consequence, and some of their voices were embarrassingly high, shrill, and silly, and I hatred them. Every now and then they would try to include me in their activities, though I wonder if this was at my uncle's prompting. We went orienteering one morning, which I didn't fully understand but had something to do with maps and a compass, and we had to walk through drizzly fields, then we went abseiling, then pony trekking, and I was put on a horse over which I had no control, and then we had to lead them to the stables and brush them down and I quite liked that part of the process. The weather had still been just as misty while we were pony trekking and the guide had assured us that had it not been so murky, then we would have seen some astonishing landscapes. It had been murky for the orienteering too. And the abseiling, which I did not take part in. I just stood at the bottom of a rock face and watched.

It was the older Scouts who fascinated me. They tended to do their own thing, and their voices had broken, and they spent a lot of time chucking, in a deep-throated kind of way as if everything suddenly had comic potential. I understood that this was because they had discovered the opposite sex, and now absolutely everything had connotations beyond the obvious. They didn't appear to worry about the weather, either. I supposed that they wanted to appear cool, by wearing t-shirts when it was raining and drizzly, and show off their hairstyles in case any Welsh young ladies should wander into the camp down from the lane and the farmhouse. Uncle had to tell them off a couple of times because of their swearing, and all I could think was, *I'll be like that very soon.*

Luke and the older Scouts were transfixing, because I could see in them the obviousness of my masculinity. There was no disguising the power they held in their bodies; you could hear it in their voices. Their playful punches would have knocked out a younger kid. They acted so carefree in each other's company, and I reckoned that this was because they had all undergone the transformation that I looked for and came out the other side unscathed. No jealousy, no competition, just a common bond of youthful power and a healthy anticipation of a life to come. I could not wait for my own metamorphosis.

33

Prolonged use of waterproof macs after a few days had started to lead to an uncomfortable and quite pungent existence. The body processes moisture at an alarming rate, coating the inside of the plastic mac with a film of condensation. Yet the rain kept on falling, and the ground became churned into a muddy swamp, and the only time I felt any comfort was when I was in my tent with the zip zipped and my soaking clothes removed in favour of the sleeping bag. By the middle of the week, I wanted to come home even if it meant returning to the noise and the music and everything else.

On the evening of the penultimate day, Uncle - or 'Skip', as I had to call him when I was with the other Scouts - lit a bonfire on the banks of the river and we were all invited to gather around and toast marshmallows and sing camping songs. Most of the Scouts were reluctant to take part, particularly as the rain had intensified and even the most dander-headed doofus among the younger Scouts had figured out that the whole week was a miserable write-off. The older Scouts flat-out refused to join in, because they said it was not cool and that this was the sort of thing that you only did in the Cubs.

'A lot of planning has gone into this trip'. Uncle – Skip – explained. 'And if you don't join in, then it just looks ungrateful'.

But then, possibly thinking of Luke and his recent bereavement, he relented and said that it was only compulsory for the younger Scouts.

They started singing. Their voices were all high and it sounded very funny, out there in the dark in the mountains. But the songs were fun and silly, and they had repeating refrains in the chorus

I hung on the periphery of the group. Around me, I could feel the darkness closing in. The mountains loomed out there somewhere as the smoke rose up and joined the mist and the drizzle. I could feel the mountains all the time, even though I could not see them, which reminded me of being at home in my room and sensing London just sitting there. And it felt like there were other things too, out there in the gloom. I could not tell if they were malevolent or not, but they were inching their way towards me. I did not know what they were, yet. I was worried that I had been wrong about the way I'd wanted my life to go.

Luke and the lads were a demonstration that it would certainly be possible to develop in the way that I'd always wanted, even if I could see no hint yet in myself. The younger Luke had once been like I was now, before his body had become long and thin and his cheekbones had developed, and his hair had adopted a trendy style that framed his eyes and made them appear like those of a wild thing hiding in a hedge. This all lay before me and I would grab it with both hands and try to ignore the nagging sensations deep within that the occasional attraction I felt for the male form was just a shot across the bows, a warning that I was straying too far.

The campfire threw long shadows. I tried to get close to the heat. The younger Scouts were all still wearing their waterproof macs and wellington boots, as was I. Something was moving out there in the dark. I had not thought that much about Luke during the week, he would just kind of been there, I had not hardly noticed him at all because the week had been so miserable.

Everyone was singing now, and I tried to join in. The rain intensified as if it, too, wanted to join in. I shrank inside my waterproof mac as I felt the darkness reach out towards me. The mountains were looming, but I could not see them. I was just taking people's word for it that they existed.

34

The morning would have started the same as all the others that week. Forsaking the warmth and dry of my sleeping bag, I clambered back into soaking wet jeans, a fresh t-shirt, and the plastic mac lined with yesterday's condensation, then stepped into my Wellington Boots, which were similarly damp and caked with mud. It was not cold - in fact, it had been mild, muggy, and humid, which made the wearing of all that plastic and rubber even more uncomfortable. But I would have shivered, nonetheless. This was the last day, though. Soon we would be going home.

And it is a day which I remember, even now.

I'd have made my way across the sodden grass to the breakfast marquee where the other Scouts would have gathered, and steam would have been rising from the metal tea mugs, and I'd have sat at a wooden bench and eaten soggy cornflakes from a tin bowl, and it was our last day so Uncle would have been talking about how we'd all have to pack up the tents and load up the Scout bus and it would all have to have been done with military precision, and I'd have been willing to take part because I was a man and I knew that it would get me away from that place all the quicker if it went well. It was a shame that I hadn't seen the Neon Yak the night before when I'd been standing at the campfire, because that would have been the ideal moment for it to have become visible through the dank and the gloom, but it had been a good idea of my Uncle's to have me come along on this trip, to toughen me up, prepare me for that moment of metamorphosis, and I'd have been thinking about all of this as I finished the cereal and went over to the washing up bowls when *something happened*

and only looking back now after forty years do I realise that this was the moment that

something changed inside of me a little bit

and the mist would have been swirling, and the drizzle and the murk would have given that camp a monochrome aspect and all the Scouts were in their waterproof macs and wellington boots because they were so sensible and yet

something was about to happen

and

something was about to change a little bit

because Luke's tent zip opened and it barely registered because his tent was out on the periphery because he'd been one of the last to arrive and in all honesty I'd tried not to even think about him during the week because I wouldn't have known what to say if we'd actually had a conversation what with his mother so recently passing away so I guess I had tried to block his existence out of my mind up until that point but his tent zip opened and I just happened to glance up and -

you'll have to understand it was sort of an incongruity, for this valley in the Welsh mountains had become nothing but a place of intense discomfort and I was a creature of the suburbs, but his tent unzipped and he crawled out and he was wearing a plain white t-shirt and a pair of shiny blue Adidas football shorts with the stripes down the side and these shorts were very short because this was the style with footballers at the time, and he *wasn't wearing anything else no coat no boots nothing else*, and I thought, surely he must be about to put on his waterproof mac and his soaked jeans and his wellington boots, but no, that was it, that was all he was wearing that drizzly muddy morning, and he started walking over to the breakfast marquee, his long long legs contrasting against the green of the grass and the brown of the mud and his bare feet sinking into the mud so carefree so different like he was walking on a tropical beach and he brushed a strand of hair from his eyes and he looked so nonchalant about the fact that he was wearing the exact opposite of what the weather dictated at that moment, and looked so incredibly handsome and so slyly sexual, and about the fact that he had made

everything suddenly changes a little bit

without him even noticing.

'Morning', he said to Uncle.

'Morning', Uncle said back.

And Uncle would not have even commented on the fact that he was dressed only in t-shirt and shorts. Because Luke was recently bereaved, and he could basically do whatever he pleased. And then, oh, as if to enforce whatever point Luke was making to the world, he *took off his t-shirt and began drying his face and hair with it,* and that bright powerful chest was there right in front of me, and I washed up my cereal bowl and mug very very slowly, and I was probably staring, and Luke would have sat ever so casually at one of the breakfast benches like it meant absolutely nothing at all, and he would have popped the t-shirt on the table surface next to him as if this was how people always acted first thing in the morning in a Welsh valley in the middle of the pouring rain in the middle of his grief in the middle of the 1980s and I remember exploding inside and wanting to go

113

home and wanting to lie down and ignore the millions of thoughts and images and ideas that were now flying around inside my head that were screaming at me that the world was wrong and I was wrong and I could just turn around from the washing up bowl and see him and that I would get so much internal satisfaction from doing so but that I mustn't, I shouldn't, I couldn't, it wasn't right and it wasn't proper and it wasn't allowed but it was very real and the world was suddenly a very confusing place, and without looking, without turning around for one more glance, I dried my cup and my bowl and I went back to my tent and I stayed there until I was sure that Luke was no longer visible.

35

Emerging from a Welsh wet tent,

a dribble of drips from the canvas lip,

surveying the dull battleship sky, this is

no place for a suburban soul, a

grimace, I'm inclined to bury myself

in adventure paperbacks or *Top Trumps*,

it's what boys are meant to do.

She's the first drag queen to scale

Everest.

My my, Ms Afterburner,

Tina to her closest colleagues,

even in those high heels and all that glitz,

your witty repartee has had us in fits.

We thought you were stranded on that ledge.

But no base camp is this. A field

sodden and trudged into a quagmire, this is

Ffarmers, you read that right, two effs, deep in the

Welsh mountains and those two effs suddenly appropriate,

it hasn't stopped raining for four long gruelling days.

You know what you can do with that second F.

It's hard to be fabulous, harder still, age twelve,

Dressed in a plastic mac and wellington booted and feeling

pretty damn miserable, this row of

Greenlander tents like the set of M*A*S*H

except without the humour, though a swamp this definitely is.

Tina Afterburner's off, she's clambering on that rock face,

in sequinned frock and scattering glitter as she goes.

She's not afraid of the Yeti. C'mon, my boy,

she yells, *don't just stand there*

with a face like a wet week in Wales,

which is what this is.

Fellow campers, classmates, Scouts, similarly

ensconced in plastic macs, this quasi-military bunch

never smelled so rank amid the pungent sweat

and constant damp, each footstep a sodden squelch,

water oozing from the clay bed fields.

'The rain just didn't stop last night', he says.

His jeans are permanently clammy, the breakfast area underneath

a canvas sheet on poles from which a constant dribble

sounds like a horse peeing for England, he imagines

Tina in her glamorous dress, she's telling him that

there's a mountain he's about to climb but he's not sure

if he wants to, I mean, will the effort be worth it?

Tina yells, 'Oh! I've come such a long way, my darlings!

Can you imagine, a small-town girl like me, all I

wanted to do was sing in a cabaret and climb Everest,

and I tell you, honeys, I've climbed a few Everests

in my time! But you never forget your first glimpse,

that time you see the mountains in all their glory!'

Scoutmaster said, 'Be nice to Luke, OK?

Don't let him know that we've had this chat, be nice to him,

His mother took her own life just a few weeks before,

he's a Venture scout, he'll be leaving us soon, but in

the meantime, everyone, give him a break,

give Luke a break'.

The rain intensifies, I help with the washing up just to feel

the warm water on my hands surrounded by the rustle and creak
of plastic pack-a-macs,

Luke, five years older than I, Luke,

defying the conventions of society, emerges late from his tent
and . .

I put down the washing up sponge, it feels like I've been slapped!

Luke hasn't bothered with a rain mac or boots, he is in

a plain white t-shirt, blue Adidas football shorts . . And nothing
else!

Long long legs stark against the mud and drab and grey granite,

bare feet, bare arms, not even a hat, he stretches,

faces skyward and embraces the rain, then saunters

over, stand with hands on hips and asks, 'Alright, lads?

Am I too late for breakfast?'

Tina's so high now she's going giddy, but she doesn't want
oxygen.

What's the point of putting on all that slap if you're

just going to cover it up with a horrible mask? Darling,

I'm here to look gorgeous, and when I get to that summit

I'm going to bellow *I Will Survive*, and it will echo in

the valley below, oh darling, have you just seen the mountain

for the very first time?

He's so much older than the others, Luke, you'd

think he'd know better, I can't even concentrate on the washing up,

he's laughing and joking now with the other ventures, these

tough tough lads veterans of canoe trips, abseiling,

tug of war, raft building, blokey pursuits, ohhh, those long white legs

pristine in the early morning gloom, I'm standing here

with my hands still plunged in the soapy water, oh look, his t-shirt

is soaked and it's pressed tight to his manly frame, oh my goodness

he's taken it off now and he's wringing it out, and he's still chatting

to the other ventures like none of this means anything and I can't

control any emotion other than this sudden morbid fascination which

does something deep within me and oh for goodness' sake doesn't

he understand what this is doing to me?

Tina's at the summit now, she's planted her rainbow flag.

It's not the first time she's ascended an obstacle, and it won't be

the last, there's glitter in the air and magic too and she flings

her arms wide, earrings swaying as she bellows,

'First I was afraid, I was petrified!'

The soft layer of muscle on bone structure, the innate masculinity

of his broad shoulders, the slender architecture of his blokey
frame,

the juxtaposition of desires one would normally associate with
the feminine

like you're supposed to with that manly manly truthfulness of
him and it's

not just Luke, no sir, if he can stir up all these emotions then
surely

there are others out there, too.

I go and hide in my tent. If I had gone missing

it wouldn't have taken long to find me in Ffarmers.

Perhaps they were shivering when they named this place.

The rain continues to fall, sounding like the crackling soundtrack

of an old black and white film as it flecks the canvas roof.

Those legs, though, that vision, why did no-one

ever tell me that this were permissible, that you could grab

such desires in all the places where people said they would never
be,

but didn't Scoutmaster say that we had to give the poor lad a
break?

The mist had been so bad all week he'd not once

had a chance even to glimpse the mountains.

'You've done it again, Tina!', they say, as she

returns to base camp, she waves to her

adoring fans, says, 'Darling, give me

a vodka martini, nothing else will suffice!'

She lights a cigarette and blows a cloud of smoke

which lingers in the Himalayan air.

4

36

I would have returned home reluctantly despite the discomfort that I had experienced during the week away. I might have been heading for a proper bed and dry clothing, but the sight of our house and our street, and the yelling of the neighbourhood kids, and the thump of unsolicited music, nullified any joy I might otherwise have had. I could not stop thinking about Luke. Why couldn't I stop thinking about Luke? The fact that he lived on the 'estate', and therefore came from the same background as myself, and yet felt so comfortable with his body as to show it off in such a brazen manner without even thinking of what effect this might have on those around him, meant that I wondered how many other surprises the universe might be hiding. It was as if he knew that his semi-naked appearance in the middle of the Welsh drizzle would stir certain feelings within his audience, purposefully subverting the breakfast ceremony, destroying my last day there, the following week, and my mind entirely, and perhaps even my life forever. Yet none of the other Scouts, nor my uncle, saw his behaviour as noteworthy in any way. Luke came to breakfast in just his shorts, I explained to one of the other Scouts. So? he had replied.

So?

I really could not stop thinking about it. Sure, Luke was recently bereaved, and people act differently at times of great emotional stress. He was determined that he would be doing things in a more subversive manner from now on and showing the world that he would be taking no prisoners, but the world had not even cared in the slightest. Apart from me.

Seeing him semi-naked had been a pivotal moment of my existence, but it was only within a couple of days that I realised I wanted more. To him, I was just a young man, not even that - a kid - dunking the same tin mug into the warm water of the washing up bowl. I was hardly even recognisable. Yet if he had let me, I would have put my hands on his bare chest and felt the warmth of his body. I would have studied him slowly, his legs, his cheekbones, his shorts. But weren't these thoughts that I should have been having about women?

I sat at my window, and I looked out at the jumble of back gardens, and fences, sheds, and hedgerows. It was sunny again, and warm now that we were back from Wales. A yellow smog haze hung in the sky over London. All the television aerials were still facing in the same direction. Within days I would be at secondary school, and it could not come quick enough because I was a little scared about what I was turning into, yet all I could think was, *Luke lives on the same estate.*

So, I went out. I didn't know what my intentions were, but I thought that I might go to the part of the estate where Luke lived. He might see me, and recognise me from the Scout camp, and we would get chatting, and he might say that it was so hot that he might take off his t-shirt again, because it was something he did when he was too hot. 'Have you ever tried it?', he might ask. And then one thing might lead to another, but I could not do the maths, I could not work out what it might lead to.

I walked out of the front door and over to the *Mr. Scott Is a Tosser* roundabout. The kid from across the street was going round it on his bike. He was about seven or so.

'Where are you going?', he asked.

'I'm going for a walk', I replied.

He laughed.

'Where are you really going?'

'I'm really going for a walk'.

'Weirdo', he sung.

I walked to the end of our road and into the road that it joined, where all the houses were of the same design as ours, and I wondered if the builders had become bored of building all these identical terraced houses, or whether they were constructed with an ideology that the people who would be living in them were going to be happy just to have somewhere to live. The road led to the next road on the estate, where the houses were of a different design because they had been built afterwards, and they had flat roofs and plate glass windows and the gardens were all open plan, though the grass had bleached almost white in the hot sun, and the ground was dusty.

It seemed nicer in this part of the estate, like the council had learned from its mistakes in the older part where I lived. People were sitting here and there in doorways or on deckchairs, older men and women chatting, kids were playing on the open plan gardens running back and forth, everyone was enjoying themselves. I was conscious that people were looking at me because they knew that this was not my road. I looked like a tourist. They might see me and realise that I was a friend of Luke's, having just come back from the Scout camp with him on the Welsh mountainside, that we had this connection. For surely, Luke's participation in the Scout camp must already have been part of the local mythology, and everyone would have been in awe of his spirit of adventure and sheer tenacity of his going in the first place so soon after his family's bereavement. Word would have got around that he had taken his shirt off. I might want to tell him that I saw them fish his mother out of the pond on the common.

The road looped back to the original one and I did not see Luke. I must have passed his house, though, and therefore his bedroom, and there's a small chance that he might have looked out of his window and seen me and realised that I was the one washing up his tin mug when he'd stood semi-naked in the Welsh drizzle, and who knows, perhaps he was similarly semi-naked right at that very moment on such a hot day, leaning against the windowsill and looking at me and thinking, *next time I see him, we'll become real good friends,*

Or maybe not, I told myself, as I turned the corner back into our road. Who would have wanted to be associated with someone from this part of the estate? The downtrodden houses huddled and joined together like footballers lined against a free kick, the shabby gardens, the windows open with music coming out from mysterious interiors, yet wasn't this my culture? Wasn't this who I was? The kid was still going round and round the roundabout on his bike and there was something mocking in his voice when he asked, 'Enjoy your walk?' And I understood that when the metamorphosis finally occurred, I would not be going for any more of these walks.

I sat down on the front doorstep. It trapped the heat. The motorway was rumbling and droning. I could hear a grasshopper somewhere, and aircraft on the runway. I could not understand why I had gone for the walk, and I was a little disappointed that I had not seen Luke. A part of me was disappointed that I had gone for the walk in the first place. What did I think would happen? The chances of him seeing me were very slim. Yet should I even have been thinking in such a way? It was time that I should start transferring the emotions I felt towards Luke on to a girl, a woman, a lady, and while it was good that I had convinced myself that I was capable of these emotions, it was sad that I had deployed them erroneously. Yet . . . Hadn't Luke looked gorgeous, let's be honest here, he had looked outstanding, and he had shaken my spirit to the core.

Should I really have been thinking this way?

The Pyromaniac sauntered in through his front gate.

'What are you doing?', he asked.

'I'm sitting in the sun', I replied. 'Isn't it obvious?'

'Oh, look at me', he said, flopping his hand in front of him using the kind of camp mannerisms of a television comedian. 'Oh, look at me, I'm sitting in the sun'.

And he was right to do so.

37

I assure you that this is true.

After my parents got married, they lived in a mobile home on a caravan site in Surrey. The site was well-laid out with little gardens and fences and a car park, and it would get so cold in the winter that frost would form inside the actual rooms, but they lived there for a few years when they were much younger. Dad would say how much he liked living there, but Mum would say that she hated it because of the cold and because of one spooky thing that happened. And this spooky thing put her off living there forever.

Dad would go to the pub in the evenings and play darts and Mum would stay behind in the caravan and read books, because there was not anything much else to do in those days, or she would listen to the radio, or occupy herself somehow. The caravans were quite large, with separate rooms, so it was quite cosy. One night it was dark, and Mum was reading a book or a magazine when, so she describes it, there was a fizzling sound and a ball of light suddenly edged through the wall, floated ever so slowly across the middle of the room fizzling and sizzling and illuminating everything very brightly, and then it merged through the opposite wall and disappeared. This ball of light lit up the room with its eerie glow, and only after it had gone did Mum start screaming and went to a neighbour's caravan and wouldn't come home until Dad had finished his darts match. Even to his last days, Dad swore blind that the ball of light was just the torch beam of a local peeping tom, but Mum said that she knew what she saw and that it definitely and absolutely wasn't a torch beam.

This story transfixed me throughout my formative years because I believed Mum's version of events and it proved to me that we did not really know everything about the world.

A few days after the end of the Scout camp, the summer ended with a fierce thunderstorm which started around eleven at night. It had been ridiculously hot and humid leading up to the thunderstorm and after I went to bed, I lay there on top of the sheets with the sweat just rolling down my body. The sky began flashing over London, sheet lighting flashing one after the other and it was all very unnerving, but I wasn't scared even though we lived on a hill, because whenever we had thunderstorms as a kid, Mum would always say that the storm 'followed the river', whatever that meant. The Thames was at the bottom of the hill, and she would say that the storm followed it along and would not hurt us even though we were on this hill next to the Thames, because the storm just wanted to 'follow the river'. And anyway, I had always been fascinated with weather and with the way that it makes the world change every few minutes.

But this storm was ferocious and even to this day, I've never known a storm like it. The sky was flashing and pulsing like a disco, and then the thunder started, and the claps of thunder were so loud that I could hear them even through my earplugs, and the house shook in a way it normally only did when Concorde took off. I could feel the storm getting closer and closer, moving right across London towards us, so I got up from my bed and I looked out and could see fork lightning splitting the sky, several zaps every second, and the loudest thunder I'd ever heard. I rested my elbows on the windowsill, but soon I started to get scared because it looked like the fork lightning was getting closer and I worried that I might get struck, so I drew the curtains, and I went back to lying on my damp bed.

You could feel that there was electricity in the air, that's the only way that I can describe it. Everything became all fuzzy. The sky was flashing, and the thunder was booming, and it seemed like every few seconds my window would be lit from behind the curtains by this natural and cataclysmic light show, and the sweat was rolling off my body. I had never known anything like it.

So what happened next kind of seemed to fit right in with the logic of the situation, because amid the crashing and the booming and the flashing there came a sizzling sound, and I became aware of what can only be described as a sphere of lightning which, accompanied by the flashes of sheet lightning and the zaps of the fork lightning, ambled its way from right to left immediately outside of my bedroom window, throwing the shadow of the window frame itself from one wall to the other, and it all made sense, and yet it didn't. And it would have floated past my window, and then the window of the kids next door, and then the window of the Pyromaniac, and then it would have sizzled off to wherever it was heading, and I didn't understand the world anymore, and yet I did.

38

A persistent rain fell for the whole of the next day. It dampened the facade of the houses across the street and made it look like they were sweating. I didn't tell anyone what I had seen the night before, but it had made me feel as if nobody had much of a right to profess to the truth. I cycled to the park and chained my bike to the fence, then walked in and took the path around the lake, wearing the same waterproof mac and wellington boots that I had worn in the Welsh mountains. I did not worry so much about getting wet, though, because the skin underneath can just dry right off. The world smelled sweet and fresh.

I did not know it at the time, but the summer had ended, and the hot days would not be coming back. I would soon have so much more to think about. The path around the lake was spongey and damp and puddles had formed between the roots of the trees. I didn't see another person walking because the rain was just so intense. Halfway around the lake, a path barely perceptible as such cut off and headed away into the woods and the rhododendrons, but I knew exactly where I was going. Wet branches scraped at my plastic hood, so I lowered it, and I let the rain fall on my hair and down my neck. I liked that feeling of just giving in to the elements. The path was unkept and I would have to clamber over roots and thorns and because of this my progress was slow, though it all reminded me of being in Wales, stepping over the guy ropes around the tents in that field next to the river.

The casual observer would easily have missed the rhododendron bush because it looked just like all the others, but it was almost like home to me by now, and I stepped away from the path and plunged myself into its foliage, bending down through the opening, and then over the familiar branches within its main body where the rain wasn't quite so intense. All the time, though, my heart was beating, beating, and when I came out out the other side into the clearing, where I'd spent so many wonderful hours reading in the sun, I felt incredibly excited.

Because this time was going to be different. I stopped moving and I listened intently, to make sure that there definitely wasn't anybody else nearby, and then, concealed by the fleshy leaves of the bush, I removed my waterproof mac, my wellington boots, my jeans, my socks, and then my t-shirt, and folded them gently, and stood there in the rain wearing the exact same brand of football shorts that Luke had been wearing.

I felt the rain on my bare shoulders. I felt every breeze on my bare flesh. I felt the muddy ground and the wet grass underfoot. I felt the weak sun behind the dense rain clouds. I felt the earth beneath me. I felt oddly sublime, because this was a sensation that I shared with Luke, we both knew what it felt like, and it was highly improbable that anyone else on the estate would share such knowledge, and it felt great. I smiled. I just stood there, smiling, letting the rain fall on me.

Just like Luke.

Who knows, I thought. If anyone saw me, then I might provoke in them the same feelings that I had had when I had seen Luke. And it was not inconceivable that even Luke himself might suddenly walk past and appear from the rhododendron bush, and say something like, 'Oh, I know how that feels. Good, isn't it?', and I would say something like, 'I was there the day they took your mother out of the pond on the common.'

I walked around the clearing. I tried to act casual, just like Luke had acted casual as he'd come out of his tent and wandered over to the breakfast marquee, I tried to act like this was something that I was used to and that I did every day, but my hands kept wandering to my shorts, or to my own bare chest, as if to remind myself that this really was happening, right here, right now, in the rain, the night after seeing ball lightning, the week after returning from Wales, the day before going to secondary school, that this was actual and it was real and that there would definitely be a next time.

Of course, I could not have stayed there forever. And when I heard voices, and footsteps, and the crashing of branches, I knew that someone was coming. I dressed as quickly as I could because I knew how suspicious it might have looked to whoever was out there. A man and a woman, from the sound of it, just having a normal conversation as they walked along the secret path which led away from the lake right past the rhododendron bush. I tried to do up the zip of my waterproof mac as quietly as I could. I waited for them to pass, and then made my way back through the bush, emerging on to the path on my hands and my knees, right in front of them.

'Oh!', the lady said.

'How weird', the man said.

And I just scampered away from there, thinking how it had been even weirder a couple of minutes previously, I just walked away as quickly as I could without even turning around. I went back to the path around the lake, and then back to my bike, and I unlocked it, and I hopped on, and I cycled back to the estate.

39

Tina Afterburner stood backstage, waiting for the curtain to open. She could hear the audience in the main auditorium. We could both hear the audience. Hubbub, excitement for the evening's entertainment, anticipation for the star of the show. Tina was wearing a blue sequin dress, high heels, a brown wig elegantly coiffured and sculpted, and dangling earrings. She stood with her hands on her hips, legs slightly apart, filled with a nervous energy I'd never seen before. Any moment now the curtain would slide open, and the audience would burst into enthusiastic applause, and she would go straight into her first number.

'Aren't you scared?', I asked.

'Honey, I'm nervous. But it is good to be nervous. It shows that you are invested in the performance'.

'But what if they glimpse the real you underneath?'

'Darling, this is the real me'.

'I shouldn't be here', I whispered.

'We all choose our theatre', she said. 'Whether we've auditioned, or not'.

'What's that supposed to mean?'

'It means I'm about to blow their socks off and when I've done, they'll have a whole different understanding of life itself'.

The music was rising to a crescendo. Tina started breathing deeply. I could see her chest rising and falling. She closed her eyes. She was listening for her cue.

'Where are we, anyway?'

'Well let me tell you, babes, this isn't Englemede Social Hall, that's for sure'.

'I won't have to do anything, will I?'

'What do you mean?'

'They won't see me, will they?'

'No'.

'Can't I just carry on the way that I am?'

Tina opened her eyes, smiled, and looked right at me.

'And how's that working out for you?'

'It's been good'.

'Seriously?'

'And it will be even better once I've seen the Neon Yak and started dating my first girlfriend'.

Tina let out a snort of a laugh.

'Why did you laugh?'

'Oh, honey . . .'.

'Why did you laugh?'

'You'll see the humour, eventually'.

A voice boomed out through the theatre sound system.

'Ladies, gentlemen and everyone! The moment you have all been waiting for! Let's have an amazing round of applause for - Tina! Afterburner!'

With that, the curtains swished open, and Tina threw out her arms wide as if she were trying to embrace the noise, the lights, the applause, the music, the excitement and the sheer spectacle of the situation, and I hid in the wings, pressing myself into the dark theatre wall where no-one could see me, I pressed myself deep into that wall.

40

Secondary school.

I had been waiting for it for so long, and now, here it was. A labyrinth of flagstone-tiled corridors and thick walls coated in layer after layer of paint. High windows to deter pupils from looking out at the world. Victorian sensibilities, Victorian solidity.

Mid-morning during one of my first lessons, a slant of sunbeam that looked almost solid illuminated airborne chalk-board dust. I put my hand out to try and touch it, much to the amusement of the lads on the desk behind mine.

There was a constant smell of leaking gas, and bleach. Polish. Aviation fuel. In between lessons the corridors echoed with thousands of footsteps, a hubbub of voices deeper than those I was used to, from people I had never met who smelled differently with their hair gels and their aftershave and their body sweat. They came from different suburbs and different schools, and they acted differently, and they supported football teams and wore coats emblazoned with unfamiliar logos. I felt that I could become so very anonymous here, and this suited me fine. Anyway, hadn't Luke once navigated these very corridors?

There were systems in place, and because of them, it felt like a factory, this sprawling collection of buildings and wings and the sports hall and the tower block built because the school had run out of room to spread out and now had to go up, up. You could see the terminal buildings at the airport from the science rooms at the top. They let you look out the windows when you were this far up.

I did not know any of my fellow pupils. They were a confusing assortment from various feeder schools to the west of

London, who exuded a sense of newness as if they had just popped into existence minutes before, we were introduced. I realised how insular my little school had been, and how we had all grown up together and become comfortable with our individual quirks and now everything had been reset, and I would have to start all over again with new people. Was this my chance to road-test a new personality, and would it, hopefully, coincide with my impending transformation? How fortuitous that would be.

It was with these new colleagues that the necessity of my impending transformation became more urgent. It was pointed out to me frequently by my new classmates that anything different from the heteronormative was to be avoided, and many reasons were given for this, not least the AIDS epidemic and the policies of the current government and the views and routines of various television comedians whose catchphrases became all the more timely when transferred to the playground environment, *backs against the wall, lads*, being an oft-repeated favourite. And I would have played along, glad that the forthcoming transformation would shield me from such barbs. Rain fell from an overcast sky, drizzling our PE kits as the sports tutor tried his best to impinge in me the correct method of winning a tackle during a football match. I never knew that such things were important. Teammates laughed at my efforts. How would I ever impress the girls with football skills as dire as mine?

41

Frost-clung sun and scratchy ear-splitting aircraft

In the cold winter morning.

The thrum and hum of motorway traffic

Filtered through classroom windows,

Chalk-dust swirling in a low-slung sunbeam.

Ricky would always be the first to arrive at the tutor group. The first to arrive after myself, that was. I was so afraid of being told off for being late that I would get to the school incredibly early. Ricky came from a village like Englemede so we both had to get the bus.

Spiky hair and

Ever-present grin.

Baby of the class,

I'd never seen

Someone so confident in the

Apparent good fortune of being

Supremely handsome,

And I hated myself for liking him for it,

And I liked him for it

A lot.

There was something fresh about Ricky. I'd never met him before so it was something of a surprise to understand that boys like him could exist. He seemed so confident in himself. There was that sense yet again that he had just popped into existence seconds before I had met him for the first time.

I looked like a ghost

Feeling old even then.

These kids would soon be men.

I'd never have to see them again.

Then in would come the lads from their

Morning kick-about,

Big-mouthed lairy boys smelling of

Hair products,

Diesel exhaust from suburban bus rides,

Cheap aftershave even though

None of them yet shaved,

Sculpted and gelled hair

Modelled on TV heartthrobs, pop stars,

Synth-pop balladeers.

These were the local kids who lived within walking distance of the school. They did not grow up in a suburban village. They were wiser to the world, or so I understood it.

Jocks and sports fans,

Deep-throat spotty jack-the-lads,

Male bimbos and the terminally odd,

Random souls thrown together by

Secondary-school scheduling,

Quoting football statistics and carrying

Sports equipment emblazoned with

Various London team logos,

The air thick with teenage hormones and

Estuary accents, mock-Cockney,

Strange sudden Americanisations they've learned

From watching imported action serials.

I could sense even at this age that there was a pressure to conform to whatever the stereotype of the schoolboy should be. They looked at the world differently. When had they seen the Neon Yak? Some of them already had girlfriends, or so they said. They were obsessed with sex and with football, but they talked about football more than they talked about sex. Only now do I

realise that they talked about the one thing that they
understood.

They joke and push and shove and they

Joke about football

And they joke about football managers

And they joke about football players

And football supporters

And I smile and I try to join in because

It's important that I join in

But I don't know what any of this means

And they laugh at me for it.

Because it seemed that the only way to prove that you were
different was to confess that football meant nothing to you.
They could not understand that this was possible, that someone
could go through their whole life so far without once deciding to
watch a match or support a team. It was inconceivable to them.
Or they already recognised the humour in the fact that I existed
outside of their universe.

Omar was in the same boat, but he had the sense

To mug up on the football results the night before

So as not to be left out.

Alan was anonymous but he was defined through

The team he supported because that was

Apparently very important.

Phil was similarly characterised though

Even now I cannot remember anything he did or said

That was remotely noteworthy.

It seemed that our class had every conceivable type of

Male representation

In the very narrow band from which

We grew up.

I made a mental note to decide to follow a team, but I really was not sure what the teams were called nor why one should be picked over another when we all lived to the west of London, near the airport. But there was more to it than just football. The lessons were hard enough, but it seemed like the greater education came from being with other lads.

Tutor group periods were a time of

Frequent laughter and boisterousness.

One of the Justins would break wind

And everyone else would laugh as if

It was the funniest, most whimsical amusement of the decade.

I probably laughed too.

I didn't want anyone to think

That I was different.

But I hated these losers

With a passion.

Not that I was being bullied, physically. They sensed that I was different, but this was not drawn to anyone's attention. I was so very tired by their antics and most of all by their noise. The tutor group classroom sounded like a riot in the long minutes before our tutor arrived.

I hated Justin's hyperactive shrieking.

I hated the way Paul would belch and then

Everyone would laugh

And others would start belching

Trying to cash in and grab some laughter

For themselves.

I hated the way that James would copy Alan's

Mannerisms

As if Alan were a philosopher of the age

Even when the thing that Alan had just done

Was downright mean and vindictive.

I hated the way that the whole lot of them would

Laugh and laugh at the stupidest things

And when they ran out of stupid things to laugh at

Then they'd start

Trawling around the room for anyone who displayed the

Slightest sign of supposed weakness,

And then the jibes would start.

Backs against the walls, lads.

Backs against the walls.

This was never aimed at me. I had done a decent job of hiding my true personality. I had done such a decent job that I had even managed to hide it from myself. Tina did not come with me to school, she stayed at home waiting for my return. I would be so embarrassed if they ever discovered that Tina existed. On the other hand I was confident that she would not be around for much longer because surely I would see the Neon Yak and then I would become at one with them, and I would find a football team to support, and I would talk about the girls the way that they talked about the girls, and everything would just slot into place, but it was just taking so, so long to happen.

I hated these kids.

I hated these boys.

Gary with his mullet.

Dan with his beef-flavoured crisps.

Wayne with his peculiar odour as if he'd

Just climbed out the river.

Justin with his runny nose.

I hated them all,

I despised them all,

But I wanted

To be

Just like them.

42

Conferred by a tap, a touch, the status of 'it', whatever 'it' is, the gym teacher's method of warming up the class on a cold Tuesday morning. White t-shirts, white shorts, snarl-lipped and brutal in the suburbs, permission granted to chase the lads who howl and scream and cower in corners, the pack afraid to be labelled an outsider and yet, as 'it', the focus of the group, hearts racing, feet slap on the wooden gym hall floor, and half an hour from now we would all be in French, such is the peculiarity of the school timetable. No-one wants to be 'it', because as soon as the status is conferred, to be 'it' is everything a young soul dreads. But you get to pick on the weakest.

Today, as well as 'it', we are going to be climbing. The 'apparatus' is pulled out on hinges, wooden ladders and ropes, and we stand there looking up at the high ceiling and it all seems very daunting, and the teacher tells us that this is potentially dangerous, but to make it a bit easier we will be doing something called 'the gate' which was only a couple of metres from the ground, and that we would have to work in pairs. My first instinct is that I do not really want to work with someone else, that I would rather work on my own, and then the teacher says that I must work with Ricky, and I don't mind this one bit. It is the first time that we have been paired for anything, and I like the idea of it.

We are shown 'the gate'. We must clamber up one side of it, reach one hand over to the other side, and flip ourselves upside down and over in one almost acrobatic manoeuvre. The gym partner must stand on the other side and help if one were to have any difficulty in performing this meaningless flip.

Ricky has long legs, just like Luke. Ricky has floppy hair, just like Luke. In fact, Ricky could have been a slightly younger version of Luke. And only now, as I climb up one side of 'the gate', do I realise the similarities. Ricky stands on the other side of 'the gate' and when I get to the top I look down, and I see him, looking up and me, smiling, his arms wide as if waiting to catch me, almost tempting me to fall.

I perform the ridiculous flip and I land right next to him, but he had obviously expected me to fall, so he steps forward and makes an attempt to catch me in his arms even though it hadn't been necessary, and his arms are around me for just a moment or two, and the gym teacher tells me to do it again and I'm only too willing and again I reach over and perform the flip and again Ricky is there with his arms wide and again I am in Ricky's arms. The gym teacher tells Ricky that he only has to try and catch me, or offer assistance, if it looks like I'm going to fall, and Ricky says that he doesn't want to see me get hurt, and it's one of the nicest things I've ever heard, and he's still got that smile on his face which hints that everything will be alright with the world.

We swap over, and it's my turn to stand on the other side of 'the gate' and offer Ricky assistance, and he clambers up and performs the flip with surprising dexterity but even so as he lands I do step forward just a touch and I put my hands either side of his shoulders, but he's far more adept at these gymnastics than I, and that's such a shame. Afterwards I told myself that I should have flung my arms around him.

In the mythology that would follow, there is no more than this to tell, for it was only later that night after a day full of lessons and a bus ride home that I realised that I felt the same way with Ricky as I had done about Luke. The way that he would stand facing up at me, smiling, arms open, eager not to see me come to any harm, made me want to spend more time in his company, made me feel the same way about him that I had felt about Luke. I could not understand why the sight of him stirred such emotions, for he was so otherwise anonymous, though maybe this was part of the attraction. There were so many others like him. But he had offered comfort. That's what made him different. He had proved that he did not want to see me come to any harm. Soon, though, I would tell myself that there was nobody else like him.

Ricky

Became my reason

For going to school.

43

An autumn squall of nothing chased the summer away. Gutter-leaves blowing end over end, skittering, unable to define from which direction the next gusts will come. It is not cold enough to shiver yet, but the body undergoes its own involuntary motions. The bus stop is made of concrete, there are small stones embedded and each one a witness to so much more than this. The bus will take me to school and to Ricky, matching the bus visiting his own suburban district, which he will ride from the other direction, just like me, and we will soon meet when they converge. It's never felt like this. I was too young to realise that the sense of elation I felt was agony. I'd strayed too far from who I should have been.

No gym that day, or PE. I could see him any time I chose because he was in my tutor group, and how cruel that was, and how brave I would have to be. If one were to dissect him atom by atom, then his constituent parts would be the same as my own. I had not been brave enough to open my arms wide when I'd stood the other side of the gym apparatus. He seemed much more dexterous than I, even though I could crawl through rhododendron bushes or levitate. Where could I find refuge if the bus didn't turn up? Ricky looking up at me in the gym, his arms wide, white t-shirt, white shorts, *come to me* he was saying. He had his own football team that he supported and was defined through the characteristics of how they had performed, lads would gibe whenever his team lost,

And I had never understood the rules of the penalty kick. The little stones in the bus stop concrete had withstood so much. We must make our own mythologies.

A roar of diesel as the bus hulks into view, around the corner from the other part of the estate, green London Country livery intent on taking me to Ricky. It chugged up the road, squeezed its way around the *Mr. Scott Is a Tosser* roundabout, drew up at the bus stop all just for me, like I meant something. The doors clattered open with a fizz of hydraulics. Tina was at the wheel.

'Hop on', she says.

44

Don't you ever talk to him.

Look but you cannot touch.

The feelings that you have for him

Never will amount to much.

Don't you even think of it,

Try not to be his friend.

Nothing will ever come of this.

One day this all will end.

Don't you dare acknowledge him,

Pretend he doesn't exist.

Every time you remember him

Curl your hand into a fist

And try to go about your day

As if he isn't there

With his beautiful face, his winning smile,

Perfect eyes, his body, his hair.

Don't you ever talk to him,

That's the scheme, the plan.

Otherwise, just how on earth

Will you get to be a proper man?

45

There were two sets of stairs either side of the tower block, one painted orange, the other painted blue. We had to take the blue set of stairs up to the very top where the science rooms were. I liked going to the science room because of the view, of course, across the rooftops in the direction of the airport, and the science room had big glass windows which let in the light.

Our teacher was Mister Ballantine. He stood at the front of the classroom as we all piled in, with his hands on his hips, the fluorescent light shining off the top of his prematurely bald head. Another one of the reasons why I liked science was that my desk was near to Ricky's desk at the back of the room, and I could look across every now and then and see Ricky. We were perched on high stools for this lesson, rather than plastic chairs. It made us all just a bit higher off the ground.

Proximity to Ricky meant that I would not be able to concentrate very well. It was very cruel having to work under such circumstances. My only respite came when halfway through the lesson, Mister Ballantine decided to show us an experiment on the big, long lab bench at the front of the room. He put on his lab coat and an oversized pair of goggles, and said, in a mocking tone, 'Gather around, children', and I wanted to laugh because it was very funny him saying this, because we were not children, but nobody else laughed. Nevertheless, we all got off our stools and stood at the other side of the long desk where Mister Ballantine demonstrated a chemical reaction and when he finished, he said something like, 'Now, run along back to your seats', like he was only pretending to be a teacher, or was a kid's TV presenter. There was something slyly ironic about him.

I went and sat down again at my desk at the back of the room and Mister Ballantine asked us to write up what we had just seen him do with the chemicals, and in the quiet that followed as we did so, he wandered around the room, one hand on his hip. I tried to think about the words that I wanted to use, but my attention kept getting distracted by the form of Ricky on the opposite desk, and Ricky looked so wonderful in the bright sunlight coming in through the wide windows of the tower block science lab. And I thought of him smiling and standing at the bottom of the 'gate' in the gym hall that time, looking up at me with his arms wide, and then I stopped to think about how gorgeous he looked and why it was that nobody else was apparently totally smitten, and the next thing I knew, Mister Ballantyne was right next to me. The words might come easier, he said, if you obviously weren't so distracted by other things.

And this made me feel very awkward and embarrassed.

Mister Ballantyne walked to the front of the classroom. Sweat was forming on my forehead because it felt like I had just been exposed. But Mister Ballantyne had said this in a soft, caring kind of way, and I did my best to write up the notes that he had asked for. The lesson ended normally with the assigning of homework, and just as we all stood up to leave, Mister Ballantyne said, 'Oh, Danny Cooper, could I see you after the class has left?'

Amid the hubbub of screeching stool legs and grabbed coats, there was an exaggerated intake of break from my fellow classmates. And my heartbeat started to become amazingly fast because I did not know what Mister Ballantyne was about to say, and it took ages for the class to pack up their bags and leave, and I knew that I was about to get told off for not paying attention.

'You wanted to see me?' I asked once everyone had left.

Mister Ballantyne smiled, and he sat on the edge of the long bench at the front of his classroom.

'If you ever want to talk to me about anything,' he said, 'then I'm here, you understand?'

I nodded. 'Sure', I said, but I did not really know what he meant by saying this. And I was eager to get back to my classmates to let them know that I had not been kept behind for a telling-off.

'Sure', I said again.

'Because I can help', he said. 'It may not feel like it, but I can help. And I know the world seems a confusing place. But I've been there too, okay?'

'Sure', I repeated.

I picked up my coat and my bag and I left.

I had no idea what he was talking about.

I should have said *thanks*.

46

The field rose up from the lane, then dropped down to a small valley, a stream, and a hedge with a stile instead of a gate. Three planks of wood crossed the stream, whose waters were clear though algae clung to the smoothed-worn pebbles. I stopped here for a while, teetering on the makeshift bridge and feeling specks of rain on my face, the cold east wind bringing with it the smell of the city, the airport, motorway pollution, and winter. I wondered how many of my ancestors may have met a scene just like this one, and how familiar it would have been to them, and whether I would have any children of my own to whom this would seem almost nonsensical. I reached over and pulled some blades of grass from the bank of the stream next to the stile, threw into the stream and watched them float away, tumbling over the rocks and the pebbles. It seemed the most logical thing to do.

Tina clambered over the stile. Her sequin dress today was a dark green, to match the green of the fields through which we were walking. Her dark black wig was vivid in the afternoon. We could have been in the countryside, were it not for the constant droning of the motorway traffic and the whining of the planes every minute or so, climbing out from the airport. Whenever they reached the Noise Abatement Zone, their engines made a curious powering-down sound which could be quite unnerving to the casual observer. I had to tell Tina more than once not to worry, that it was quite safe. But by now we were talking about Mister Ballantyne.

'There's long been rumours about him', I explained. 'His mannerisms. Have you noticed? Remarkably like Mister Scott's. And you know what they used to say about Mister Scott, don't you?'

'I never met him', Tina said. She was now half-over the stile and had paused as if she were riding a wooden horse.

'But our class was with Mister Scott all day, every day. We are only with Mister Ballantyne twice a week. And it's not like he's one of the most popular teachers'.

'What does that mean, honey?'

'Mister Clarke. Mister Berry. You know, the ones that everyone likes'.

'So, nobody likes Mister Ballantyne?'

'Because of the . . . Rumours'.

'Honey - I'm having difficulty understanding you'.

I let out a huff. I hated having to explain myself.

'The boys in the class impersonate him. They used to impersonate me, but now they impersonate Mister Ballantyne, and I must admit, I join in, because it's like they're only pretending to be nasty with me, but not with Mister Ballantyne'.

'They actually are being nasty?'

'But it's OK with him, because he's a teacher, see? And he probably goes home to his wife every night and he doesn't even understand that everyone is laughing at him, so I don't see . . I don't see why . .'.

'Hang on. I'm not getting the logic, dear'.

'I don't see why he should say that he can help me with anything, because it's his fault that he's got this reputation for being different from all the others. And anyway, surely the school would not have employed someone if they weren't totally normal?'

'Whatever that is'.

Tina had now joined me on the makeshift bridge.

'What do you mean by that?', I asked.

Tina just shrugged.

'So', I continued, 'I don't know why he should say that he can help me, and anyway, help me with what? He's a comedian, you know? Like the ones on television. The impersonation the boys do of him sounds just like the impersonation comedians do on television of - you know - *gay people*. So he's just trying to be like one of those television comedians'.

'Perhaps you are, too'.

'Funny. I'm not pretending to be anyone. Not like Mister Scott, or Mister Ballantyne. Everyone laughs at them. But they're just being silly, aren't they? Making people think that they might be . . . *Gay*'.

'Honey. Darling'.

'Yes?'

'You really should take a good look at yourself'.

'What's that supposed to mean?'

'Your life. The way you think. The things you do'.

'All pretty normal'.

'The people you are . . . Attracted to'.

'The right girl hasn't come along just yet, but as soon as she does, and as soon as I see that Neon Yak . .'.

'Ricky'.

I could not help myself.

'What about him?!'

'You are in love with Ricky'.

'No, I'm not! I don't know what you're saying or why you're saying these things. That's not love! He's just the sort of person I'd like to spend the rest of my life with, because he's absolutely gorgeous and has a wonderful personality and he makes my world come alive and I ache to see his face and I want to be noticed by him and I cherish every word he says to me and I want to be with him all the time and I want to grow up and grow old with him and I want to make sure that nothing bad ever happens to him and I want to hold his hand and I want to see him naked and I want to share my innermost thoughts and emotions with him, but that's definitely not love'.

'Then what is?'

'Getting married and having kids. And anyway .. '.

'Yes?'

'He's a . . . Man. And I'm not allowed to love a man, nobody is, unless they're a woman. You know that. It's the law of the land, and it's in the Bible, and it's disgusting that some people think like that, and frankly, I'm not even sure that gay people even exist. Not real ones. Not like . . .'.

'Not like who, dear?'

'Not like .. You see, these feelings I have for Ricky, and others like Luke, and these thoughts I have, well, that's not being gay. That's something else, which has only even happened to me, and I'm the only person to feel this way, and the only person who has ever existed who has ever felt this way, and I know it's a bit

weird but it will all go away in the end, I'm pretty sure of it, and . .
Hey, what are you doing?'

'I'm fading', Tina said.

And she was. We were still standing there on those wooden
planks across the stream together, and she was now see-
through.

'Why are you doing that?'

'Honey, you'll understand one day. You don't need me
anymore'.

'I never asked for you in the first place'.

'Nobody ever does. But now you've got to get back home,
haven't you? Because you've got some sums to work out'.

'My maths teacher didn't set any homework'.

'Not those sorts of sums'.

'Tina. Stop fading'.

'I can't help it, darling', Tina replied.

And then she disappeared altogether.

'Tina?'

Tina was nowhere to be seen.

'Tina?'

I looked around. Not even a glimpse of sequin. The world
just looked so normal. The only thing in it that was out of place
was me.

47

Hard-worn sleep against the usual noise. Next door's kids playing up, crashing, and banging. Someone else's music was a thumping beat despite the muffling effects of my earplugs. Trying to find the ethereal in a world too tactile for dreaming.

Cut away the nonsense and the main characteristic of every homosexual is . . .

Here I go again, thinking about this.

But it's the nonsense that defines their place in the world, all that posturing and flouncing and femininity, do they only do it to put a purposeful barrier between themselves and the world?

But cut away all that and the main . . . The main attribute . . . Trait, if you will, is . . .

It's been said so often by those who one must abide that even to contemplate it must be wrong, because it's against everything that decent society has ever . . .

Here I go again, thinking about this.

But it's not like I'm . . I mean, I'm different, because I never made a conscious effort to sit down and think, *oh, I believe I shall fancy men now*, did I? I'm sure they do it just for shock value.

So cut away all the . . . Attributes that one would associate with the common homosexual and . . .

OK, so the thing is, what if all those people we obey and listen to and take notice of and all those rules and regulations and morals and all that public opinion and those politicians and those television comedians and those religious leaders and our old headmistress and the vicar and . . . I mean, it's funny when you think about it, but . . .

Here I go again, pondering on this.

What if they were all wrong?

No, no, no, it's just too silly to comprehend, because there have been so many centuries of thought on the subject, and it's not as I say it's not like I made a conscious effort one day to sit down and think, *oh, I shall forego any attraction I have to the opposite gender, because . . .*

They can't be wrong.

Backs against the wall, lads!

One for each person and one for the pot.

Like I'd find any of them attractive, the guys from my class, they don't understand the nuance, that's what makes it so funny whenever they say that, because none of them would ever appeal to me - I mean, obviously, apart from Ricky.

So, in essence I'm different to the common homosexual, I'm . . . There's only been the one of me in existence, so I cannot just jump into the mind of a heterosexual man, and I never asked for this, but the Bible says . . . Or does it? If anyone says I'm wrong to be myself with no actual decision committed on my part to be the person who I am, then - oh, there I go again, assuming myself to be, you know, like Mister Scott, or . . . Possibly Mister Ballantyne, for example.

Here I go again.

(Surely, he goes home to his wife?)

Backs against the wall, lads!

And I've never felt the need to flounce, sashay, wear lipstick, dress in drag, have floppy hands, speak camp, so that means, if you cut away all of that, as you might theoretically do with those who *do* have those characteristics, then . . . The only correlation, the only conclusion to be drawn is that -

Though it's just so stupid, because men were meant to be with women, it's the expected outcome in all this, but the idea of it, the idea of physical proximity to the female form churns my stomach in the same way that certain foods might, it's just that I've been confused, and there was no conscious effort, but I'm meant to be with a woman and that's what's demanded by family and society and because I've been so wrong about so much in the past, then I could very well be wrong about this, isn't that what growing up is all about?

Again, though, if you strip away all the attributes, the characteristics, the traits of the stereotypical homosexual, then . . . Then the most defining mark of any conceivable difference is . . . Loving the same gender.

And I love the same gender.

Therefore, that means I must be g

G

Grateful that no-one has ever found out, (phew!), and I must hide this forever or live a life of lying but no no no I've just done the sums wrong and now I must go back and look at my working out and and and

I must be myself, and *this* is myself. And I'm not the only one who has ever been, even if I'm the only *me* that's ever been, which means . . .

Here I go, thinking about this.

164

48

The whole world has vanished. And I am now in space. I can still breathe even though I am now in space. The planet, Earth, has vanished, and it looks like I am the only person left. And yet, I am not floating. I can feel that I am on solid ground.

The stars are all around me, but it isn't beautiful. It is quite sinister. I put my arms out and neither of them touches anything, surrounded as I am by the emptiness of space. I look down and I see that I am standing on a very thin strip. The strip looks like it has been made from the ground. What is this strip that I am standing on? And when the realisation comes, it does so with shocking force. The thin strip, which stretches away from me into the darkness, and stretches behind me into the darkness, is all that that remains of Planet Earth.

I wake with a start, and I get out of my bed in an instant. I am sweating all over, but the weird thing is that the dream is still going on. It's fifty / fifty now, I don't know which reality is correct, the one in which I am in my bedroom, or the one in which I am standing on a thin strip in space. On one side I was standing with my arms outstretched like a tightrope walker. On the other, I am now pressing myself into the corner of my bedroom, reaching out my hands and feeling the walls with my sweaty palms, pressing them in to to to to convince myself that this is the real, the physical, that the world hasn't been stretched out into a very thin strip, that I am the only human being left in existence.

The world comes back to me, and I gasp. I have never felt so relieved. I have honestly never felt so relieved.

49

The next evening, I cycled to a patch of woodland on the outskirts of Englemede. I'd never been there in the dark before, and once the sun had set the darkness gathered and seemed to seep from the trees themselves. I'd only walked a few metres into the woods, but there, surrounded by oaks and yews and brambles, I could have been anywhere, were it not for the sound of the motorway and the occasional glimpse through the overhanging canopies of passing aircraft.

I looked around a couple of times to see if Tina was with me, but I was unaccompanied. I was on my own, now. I laid my hand against the trunk of a tree feeling the rough texture of the bark, and I tried to imagine the tree talking to me, or the voices of my ancestors using the tree as a conduit, but there was nothing. The problems I had were so unique that no spirit could offer advice. But it was not advice that I was there for, nor solace, nor Tina.

If my calculations were correct, then I had no right to be there. I would not see the Neon Yak now, for such would be forever denied, through no fault of my own. I would not see its flanks glowing, floating in and out of the tree trunks, lighting the ground and the air as it wandered its solitary path. The night would not become luminous, nor would I be blessed by its hot breath on my neck. Yet here I was, just in case. Here I was in the forest. I had never been good at mathematics. I might have got it all wrong.

Did I not have every right to be there, though? I had a duty to myself to seek the truth. I took a few steps deeper into the woods and I heard the leaves rustling as I walked, pushing them aside with each step as I shuffled along the forest floor. And I thought of how it must have been thousands of years before when the land was nothing but dense woodland. It would have been just like this, it would have been autumn, and it would have been dark, and humanity had always managed to drag itself along, it's just that some histories have always been more important than others.

Deeper still into the woods. It felt as if I were walking down a hill. Wouldn't it have been amazing if I'd come across a whole town I'd never seen before? A whole town with houses and streets and cars that nobody had ever told me about, where the forest hung there on the periphery holding the darkness within, and bright lights and neon lit the pavements, and people went about their business, where I would be totally brand new and able to start with a clean slate? And I'd appear from the woods and people would smile and wave, and it would be so quiet, like it was at my grandmother's house. And the first person I spoke to would laugh and say, *oh, the Neon Yak? We have no need for it here.*

A breeze rustled the leaves and brought me back to my senses. I stopped walking and I stood still and silent. The trees were dark shapes in the gloom, and I started to wonder if I had got myself lost. How funny that would be, I told myself. To find myself lost so near to home, so near to the city that I could look at but never touch. If that was the case, then hadn't I been lost my whole life? I must be patient, I decided. Haven't I been patient, too, since the day I was born? Patient and lost. The truth is often so easy, so clear, that it can be hidden from all. And now here I was searching for it, looking in all the most unlikely of places. Why was I looking for something that might be right in front of me? Why was I trying to escape from a world that I had never been a part of? What did it matter, so long as I knew the truth of the situation.

I would have loved the woodland creatures to come to my aid. But there were none. No rabbit for me to follow laughing down into its surprisingly capacious burrow. No fox to jeer the night yet offer learned advice. No flame-vixen. No badger to snuffle the leaves and speak in aphorisms. No timid deer mysterious. The mice did not encircle me, nor chatter with excitement of missed chances and how the world moves on. Nor did I meet a wizened local in a pointed hat and trousers held up with string who would take a draw on his pipe and lean back and say that so many others of my kind had come this way, oh, so very many others. Nor did I stumble into a misty glen filled with hares, stags, and voles who sang and danced and took me by the hand in some kind of Disney approximation of sudden self-belief. None of these happened. The night just stayed dark.

I didn't know what the time was, but I figured that I should start to go back to my bicycle and head home, for surely my parents would be wondering where I was. But it was quiet out here in the woods, and the birds were singing, and I could hear an owl somewhere, and the bats were flitting about, zigzagging across the sky, and none of them cared one way or another. The owl was looking for mice. The birds wanted insects. Everything just fit so neatly together except for me. And they didn't care in the slightest.

I retraced my steps and felt embarrassed at how close I had been to my bicycle. It was either that, or time had done something weird while I was in the woods. An aircraft passed overhead, surely one of the last of the evening. I saw its lights flashing as it rose up higher and then off to whatever part of the world it called home. I waited until the sound of its engines subsided. My bike was still there, chained to a road sign, and nobody had even noticed. Or if they had, then they had decided that it was of no consequence.

50

Tentative

not for who we might become

but who we

might be.

The air

fizzes

with a truth

so rare

that it might remain hidden.

So many viable options,

paths in a forest, and

that sensation of hanging,

gathering information, and

magic, too,

drizzle like concepts

or words

in a dictionary.

The moment

a label is applied,

it's compulsory that one

live up to those

characteristics,

if only to reassure

those looking from the outside

that they were right

all along.

51

I wanted to start our chat by saying, *I think I might be like you.* And then perhaps he would yell me of a way out, an escape that was kept a secret in case too many people cheated the system. I wanted to say, *I think I might be like you, tell me how I can change this, tell me how I can alter myself*, but I was afraid of the answer. He would say that it was impossible, wouldn't he? He would say that there was no escape, that one cannot even comprehend changing the system. He would be sympathetic and tell me that I was on my own. Or perhaps – and how exciting this would be! – he might confirm that Ricky was the one for me. *Oh, good choice! And do you know what? My magical senses detect the same in Ricky that I see in you. And the two of you will live happily ever after!*

Hold on, Ricky. Hold on, I'm coming.

My day had started so normally with the usual wait for the bus, but it was only when I was halfway to school, looking out of the bus window at the car park around the supermarket in the next town, and at the people who were parking their cars and fetching shopping trollies and going about their business - old couples ambling along together - that I remembered that Mr Ballantyne had suggested I have a chat with him. As the bus got nearer to the school, I started to feel nervous because I had not known what he wanted to say, or if I was in some kind of trouble, or he wanted to expose me to the whole class and make me a laughingstock. As soon as the bus arrived, I jumped off and I plucked up the courage as I climbed the blue staircase to the very top of the tower block, to his science classroom, and I lingered outside the door, and I took a few deep breaths, and I remembered the old people I'd seen in the supermarket car park and how they had lived their lives, and fallen in love and found their places in the world, and then I went inside. He was preparing equipment on the work bench at the front of the room. He looked up when I came into the classroom.

'I think . . I need . . I hope you don't mind . .'.

'Are you okay?'

'I think I might be like you, and . .'.

'Yes?'

'And . . And you said we could chat, and . .'.

He smiled. This was new. I'd hardly ever seen him smile. He always seemed so serious when he was teaching us.

'Oh, I'm quite busy at the moment, can this wait until later on?'

Later on. Sure. What did another day matter? We arranged that I should back after the last lesson, and then I spent the rest of the day worried. What had I done? What was I about to do?

I could not concentrate for most of the day. The different lessons merged into a meaningless whole. At lunch, I could barely eat. I sat at a table and looked at my sandwich, because my stomach was churning over and over. Ricky was sitting with the lads, and he had a big grin on his face, and they were talking about football. Football was a secret bigger than my own, with its indecipherable codes. One day, I thought, he would share them with me. When the last lesson of the day finally lumbered to a close, I was the first out of the door, fighting through the corridors and the home time-bound, worried that Mr Ballantyne had forgotten about our arrangement.

He waved me in the perched himself on the edge of the workbench at the front of the science room. He gestured that I sit on one of the wooden stools.

172

'Of course,', he said, 'strictly speaking, I shouldn't be talking about these things. There's government legislation, you see. And this school is very masculine, isn't it? Which still makes me a little afraid, even after all of these years'.

'I . . I know'.

'They're just being boys. It's all a matter of education. They haven't seen enough of the world, but they're starting to act as if they have'.

We were both quiet for a bit.

'Is there anything you would like to ask me?', he said.

'There isn't'.

Which was a lie. But I was used to lying. There were lots that I wanted to ask him, but I had been conditioned into being made to feel that it wasn't proper, that it wasn't what people spoke about or admitted. And he was about to say something else when I interrupted him and I said, 'I don't feel attracted to girls, I feel attracted to boys', and saying this made me all hot and I started to sweat, and I thought that I was going to faint.

'It's OK', he said.

And I'm still embarrassed about this now, but I started to cry. And I was crying because he wasn't angry, and he hadn't recoiled in shock, and he hadn't shouted or said that he would have a word with my parents, he'd just said 'it's OK' in a calm tone of voice, in a really caring tone of voice, and I think that the tears were more a sign of relief, and he hopped off the edge of his workbench and went to his desk and to his box of tissues next to the framed photo of someone I recognised, and then he came back and handed some tissues to me and he smiled very sweetly and said, 'You're not the first kid I've had this conversation with, does that surprise you?'

And I'm even more embarrassed at my response to this.

'Was one of them Ricky?'

He laughed.

'The Rickys of this world are already set on their journey. Don't go chasing after the Rickys. You'll get nowhere, believe me'.

I tried to laugh, but this made me feel really sad.

'I've never told anyone this before'.

'We can't all be the same. Life doesn't work like that. Some people have longer legs. Some people have brown eyes. Some people are homosexual. We happen to live in a society in which intolerance is common, and that it is spurred on by newspapers and the government and religion. As a result, those who are different are made to feel that they are somehow transgressing, and spoiling it for the majority, and they are made to hide away or feel that they must disguise who they really are from the world, which only leads to heartbreak and loneliness.

'I know how it feels to pretend to be someone else. I've been there, and I used to do exactly that. The whole time, I was looking for a way out, and for attractions and relationships which did not exist. After a while – and it was a long while – I learned to relax a little bit more and go with the proper relationships which came about naturally and submit to the feelings that were deep within myself.

'The thing is, you're at an age in which the impulse is to find love. When I was the same age as you, I knew that this would be extremely difficult if I didn't know who it was that I was meant to be loving, or that if I did, then society kept telling me that I was wrong. The same is probably true for yourself. The chance of finding someone will feel insurmountable, but it will come. That's the good news. It will happen.

'You're not the only one. That's the other good news. There are so many others who have found themselves in the same situation, right now, possibly in this school right at this moment. And it is natural. It's a part of nature that they are drawn to the same gender. There are others like you – like us – and more than you think'.

His words were a comfort.

'I went through everything that you're going through now', Mr Ballantyne said. 'I know exactly how it feels'.

We both sat in silence for a while. I was on a high wooden stool, facing him. The science classroom seemed just the same as it had always seemed except there weren't any of my classmates there. The desks and the walls seemed real enough, but everything else was swirling around. It was starting to get dark on the other side of the plate glass windows, dusk gathering from the overcast skies over the capital.

'So, what you're telling me', I said, 'Is that there's no way out. That there's no escape, that this is who I am, and while it's not wrong to be that sort of person – even if so many others will make me feel that it it – that I will not be able to pretend otherwise'.

He smiled.

'You can pretend. But you would not be being true to yourself'.

'And this is who I am?'

'Yes', he said.

I started to feel very disconcerted. How could I possibly go about my daily business, and deal with the other members of my class, and my family, and my neighbours, and my Grandmother, and the pyromaniac, and the kid who rode his bike round the Mister Scott Is A Tosser roundabout, and the bus driver, and Ricky, and everyone else that I met on a daily basis, now knowing that I had been telling a lie all of these years? How would I deal with myself? How could I do schoolwork, and navigate bus timetables, and ride a bike, and read books, and watch aircraft take off and land, knowing that I was doing so through eyes which found the wrong gender - the same gender - my own gender - attractive?

'Then how had all those politicians and church people and comedians and newspapers and school kids and members of my own family have been so utterly wrong?', I asked.

'Because they are in the majority. And they speak from a position of power. And they speak from a position of privilege. And because they are – well, nasty people'.

'Really?'

'Or else, they do not understand, and they have no empathy. That's the main problem. That people really do not understand, and nor do they want to'.

'Does that matter?'

'Yes', he said. 'Yes. It matters a lot'.

I looked at the clock on the wall. It was time to go home. I had a bus to catch.

'Everything will be okay', he said. 'It may not feel like it now, but you will discover the person that you are. It is perfectly valid to have had the emotions that you have been experiencing, even if it felt like your life has been a bit weird lately'.

I wanted to ask him how he knew that my life had felt so unusual for the last few months. He understood more than I thought. He asked me if I wanted some more tissues and I said yes, and just as he went to his tissue box again, I saw the framed photograph of the middle-aged lady on his desk and I asked who she was.

She looked familiar.

'That's me', he laughed.

'But . . .'.

'Yes, I know. I'm in drag. That's my secret identity. I'm not a science teacher all the time, you know? I also perform at nightclubs some evenings, in London. I am a singer. My stage name is Tina Afterburner'.

'Tina . . .'.

'Yes, I know. Silly, isn't it? So, when I'm teaching, I keep that picture there to remind me that I have this secret existence'.

'You're Tina Afterburner?'

'Yes', he replied. He then started speaking in Tina's American accent. 'Honey', he said, 'you sound surprised'.

Which is the last thing I remember him saying, all those years ago. And I'm not sure, but I do have a recollection of stopping on the landing on my way out, looking out of one of the windows there on the top floor at the suburbs down below, one last attempt to see if anything were moving between the houses lighting each one as it went, throwing out a luminous glow, but my mind was elsewhere, and it's been there ever since.

52

This is who I am.
The only trick that nature pulled
was to instil shame in me.
I'm still a human.
There were childhood days of sun,
but this isn't playtime,
it's very real.
If I could change the way I feel
just to please others, I would.
I didn't stray once.
The path is as obvious as it always was.

I will not sully existence
or other people's morality.
The touch I crave is not alien, nor supernatural,

but human.
I'm not the first to feel this way,
even if I am the only me.
Why would anyone

prefer a soul

to be lonely?

This is who I've always been.
There was no switch,
I didn't press a button

marked with unwitting defiance,
I was not inspired by soap opera shenanigans,

nor whims, nor fashion statement,

the suburbs did not catch fire

because I managed to transgress whatever manly

aspirations are normally thrust on the masculine.
I've never sought undue attention,

and this is not the start of it.
Hello.
This is me.

It's hard to believe there are still some

who would prefer

it would never be addressed,
who favour an alternative story.
It hardly makes a difference.
I can only think that they hope
I was the only one who didn't know.

This is who I always will be

and continue to be with a pride

that came hard-won.

The comfort, solace, tutelage,

charity, benevolence, humour,

honour and respect

of generations past

live on still in me and will do always,

that I should exist in each moment

wrapped up in the man who was created and

presented to the world

with satisfaction and with love.

This is who I am.
And while I cannot understand

those who likewise cannot,
I can certainly look them in the eye
With absolute truth.
The only trick that nature pulled

was to instil them with their own hate.

53

So many years have passed since the events of this book that I'm not even sure of being the same person. Looking back, I understand how unprepared I was for the world. It surprises me that I was able to navigate a social period in which homophobia was prevalent, and attitudes were less accommodating. And it wasn't *that* long ago. Suffice to say that I have lived and loved, and subsequently, become much more comfortable with my own sexuality.

I spent four years at school with Ricky and never once told him how I felt. We grew up and became young men in that place, and while Ricky did not act quite as lairy or as boisterous as the other lads, I suspected that he would have been appalled at my attraction to him. Mr Ballantyne left after a couple of years to go to another school, and I felt a little relieved, because it took away a figure of fun that the lads in out class could easily latch on to, and the subject of his homosexuality, and it saved me from the embarrassment in his lessons of pretending that we had not had our chat. However, every now and then he would ask if I were okay, and I would always nod and say yes, and he would nod and smile, as if an understanding had passed between us.

When I left school, I never saw Ricky again. He went off to his part of the county to carry on with his life, and I did the same. I got a job at a supermarket and Ricky was replaced in my affections by a co-worker called Simon. We would have our break together, and Simon always gave the impression that he would be more receptive to my affections than Ricky had ever been. But then Simon left to go to university, and I would never see him again, either.

A couple of years after this we moved to Devon. I was sad to say goodbye to the woods and the trees and their comforting darkness, but I was excited to be leaving the suburbs behind, and the noise, and the estate. I still hadn't been brave enough to tell anyone who I was, but I thought that this might be easier in a more relaxed environment. We moved to a small fishing port on the south coast of Devon, on a peninsula that sticks out into the sea so that it really does feel like the far end of the universe. They had their own myths and legends down here, which meant that nobody had heard of the Neon Yak.

I had three glorious love-affairs, spread over a fifteen-year period. My first partner was a supermarket shop assistant, in whose company I began to sense that my life could easily be fulfilled. I also understood that my own conception of love had been based on an egotistical premise that such relationships existed only for my own gratification, and that being with someone really was a partnership. I could easily have spent the rest of my life with him, but it had all happened too soon. I then spent some time with a Lithuanian who worked in a factory where they cooked Cornish pasties, and he was a completely different kind of person, but his concept of love was similar, and we parted on good terms. I then spent an exceedingly long time with a nurse, whose view of the world was much more rounded than my own and in whose company I felt safe, and loved, and complete, and we still see each other often, and he might just be the love of my life. I realise now that I have become the sort of person that I had always wanted to be.

Forty years have passed. By chance, I became a writer of comedy shows, and a few years ago I created a theatrical solo show which took as its basis the mythology of the Neon Yak. I toured it around the country, and I took it to the Edinburgh Fringe, and each performance took me back to a very distinct time and place in my life. I called the show *In the Glare of the Neon Yak*, and it always made me think of that moment standing blindfolded in the forest and that mysterious glow being right next to my face. How close I had come to seeing that mythical beast!

It was while touring this show, lying on a bed in a Bristol city centre hotel, that I stumbled on a social media post about my old school, and I saw that one of the comments on a particular story was from someone called Nathan Ballantyne. I was overjoyed to realise that this was my former science teacher. I had often thought about him over the years, and wondered how he had navigated the decades, and what it must have been like to be a young, gay man in the 1980s teaching at secondary school. I sent him a private message, already excited and wide-eyed with the post-show delirium which always comes after a performance, and he replied to say hello, and that he was now a hotel manager in Spain, and that he clearly recalled his time teaching at the school because it had been his first full-time position after leaving training college. Which meant – I realised with a start – that he had really been quite young when he had been our science teacher. It's always difficult to judge someone's age when you are young yourself.

I asked if he remembered me, and I was a little sad when he replied that he really couldn't place me. Had I really been so forgettable? I told him about our chat, and how important that had been for me, and he said that he had had lots of chats with students back then, almost all of whom were struggling with their sexuality. The other teachers at the school, he said, had been incredibly supportive of him, and he had been the only 'out' gay teacher the school had had at that point. I asked if he still performed as Tina Afterburner and he replied that yes, Tina still made the occasionally appearance, and that she was still fabulous.

I'm writing this on a wet and windy autumn day, looking out the bay window of my rented flat in Devon. I live in a quiet neighbourhood with a park at the end of the road. I recognise that the world is a different place now, and I'm thankful for that, because there have been so many advances in society, and much better representation in the media, and that laws have been passed which benefit my community, but I also know that there are parts of the world where ignorance and intolerance are still major factors in limiting the free expression of true love. What this means is that I have been very lucky with my life. I've been very lucky indeed.

www.ingramcontent.com/pod-product-compliance
Lightning Source LLC
Chambersburg PA
CBHW030125260626
47156CB00008B/2791